7/24

our long
marvelous dying

ALSO BY ANNA DEFOREST

A History of Present Illness

our long marvelous dying

ANNA DEFOREST

Little, Brown and Company
New York   Boston   London

Copyright © 2024 by Anna DeForest

Little, Brown and Company
Hachette Book Group
1290 Avenue of the Americas, New York, NY 10104
littlebrown.com

First Edition: July 2024

Little, Brown and Company is a division of Hachette Book Group, Inc. The Little, Brown name and logo are trademarks of Hachette Book Group, Inc.

The publisher is not responsible for websites (or their content) that are not owned by the publisher.

The Hachette Speakers Bureau provides a wide range of authors for speaking events. To find out more, go to hachettespeakersbureau.com or email hachettespeakers@hbgusa.com.

Little, Brown and Company books may be purchased in bulk for business, educational, or promotional use. For information, please contact your local bookseller or the Hachette Book Group Special Markets Department at special.markets@hbgusa.com.

ISBN 9780316567121
LCCN 2023933314

Printing 1, 2024

LSC-C

Printed in the United States of America

our long
marvelous dying

A Real Calling

On my first day of work I meet a man with psychic abilities. Like what, I ask him. It is visions mostly, he says. He says in fact he had a vision in the scanner just now. The test is called an MRCP. It uses radio waves and magnets to map the course of the bile ducts. The man has cancer of the pancreas. He is in a bed in a hospital and I am beside him, a little above him, sitting on a window ledge because there are no chairs. Whenever he refers to the test, he calls it by name, as though to show me he knows what is going on. But he gets the letters wrong after the starting *M,* and the string of letters gets longer and longer every time he says it. I turn him back to the visions. Yes, whenever I start to tell one, my wife will shout at me: No, Henry! She does not want to hear it; she does not want it said. What do you see, I ask him. There is no way to know in advance if the question will come out condescending or ringing with true interest. I can only hope I hit the right note. He looks at me as though he is looking into a camera. Disaster, he tells me, catastrophe. Tell me more about that, I say, but he won't.

Whenever I notice the faults of others, I make myself imagine, really imagine, to the edge of true belief, that I too have enormous faults that are obvious to others yet completely unknown to me. Of course I don't really believe it. Enough like anyone, I am sure in my heart that, for unclear reasons, I have a slight moral edge on the rest of the world, that I am more giving and more fair and more kind. Examining this belief—knowing that it is common to most people and so cannot be true for most and so likely is not true of me—somehow does little to change it. In my case, though not always in others', the belief does seem to force me to improve the way I comport myself, to try to rise to this internal expectation, to be better, to be more generous, to cover up the lie.

Perhaps that is why I am here when I could be paid better to lead a happier life in another, more curative specialty. I am training to be an expert in pain unto death—or quality of life, as we are being trained to call it, burying the lede, elevating the plus side so patients will be willing to talk to us. I set off on this course a long time ago, and I find the reason I give for choosing it changes as I go along. Still, I recite it to myself and others until we believe it. This new world, this death, this broad, waving pandemic death, is not what I thought I signed up for. It has given the work in medicine at times the cast of a punishment. What are you saying, Eli asks when I say things like that. Eli is the man I married. He likes to remind me that cause and effect are neither targeted nor punitive, that the forces of the world have nothing to do with me.

Eli did not want to come back to the city. Some people want to live here only once. Eli hoped for us to move into a life that was less precarious, less expensive, to move away from survival living and how it makes us think only of ourselves. Or am I making that up? All he said at the time was that this life was not his own. And I feel it could go on like this, he said, for some time, for our whole lives, you going and me following along. What do you want? I meant instead. But this was never a question he could answer. Even I did not get to pick where we would end up—it was a match, fellowship, like residency was, a ranked, algorithmic assignment to another year's work. But I did the ranking. We could not agree on the order, and we took long walks about it and had a few drinks to talk it through, and the talking got heated and did not clear things up. It came to seem that he needed me to want something I did not want. I could never put a finger on exactly what it was. In the end I wrote the list in the order I wanted and submitted it without his consent.

All of the apartments we can afford are grim and lifeless with thin walls and low windows, places that remind me of places I lived when I was poor. In the suburbs we had a mezzanine duplex with a fireplace on the ground floor. I would stand staring at the fire from above with a solid sense of grandeur roaring in my heart. It was a rental, sure, but still that word *mezzanine* set me far apart from something in life I hoped never to get close to again. Now in the city, we need space for the new suburban aspects of our shared life: a midsize dog, a dozen potted plants, a child. Not ours. At last we find a place in a prewar building along a park at the very northern end of Manhattan, where, because of a lack of developmental interest, there are woods, real woods, hundreds of acres right across the street. This is the forest where the Lenape sold Manhattan for buttons at Shorakapok, *the waiting place,* now a rock with a plaque where a tree once stood. The apartment is ground floor and dark, the least of many evils.

The plants start to die right away. Someone across the alley in the back runs purple lights night and day to keep whatever he is growing alive. We will not do that, but we have one sunlamp, bright white, twelve hours on and twelve off, that the plants crowd around like lepers at the hem of a preacher. If you dust the leaves like you are supposed to, they fall right off, two down for every one left hanging. Before this, before even the first week is up, there is a flash flood and a tornado warning at the same time, piercing alerts through the cellular phone: SEEK HIGH GROUND and SHELTER IN A BASEMENT. On a hill and a ground floor, I do neither. I mute the alarms on my phone and sit at the chess set with the child, Sarah, my brother's daughter, whom he has left with us. Sarah always tries to misuse her pawns, to move sideways, attack backward, although by now I know she knows better. Eli is at work. After Sarah is in bed, I watch the cyclone tear through the tristate area on the TV news. The flood drowns tenants in basement apartments throughout the outer boroughs. Later, in Queens, I meet a woman in her thirties who is dying of lung cancer, living in such a basement with her son, who looks just shy of middle-school age. She speaks only Bengali, but her T-shirt says in English across the chest: TOMORROW IS ONLY A RUMOR.

I am trailed everywhere I go by a supervising attending. When you asked about the visions, she asks, what was the therapeutic intent? To show that I believed him. Though this answer is both untrue and insufficient. On my feedback sheet a few weeks later, hardly anonymous, I read: Interview style is somewhat hard to follow. The first attending is a palliative nephrologist. She is an expert in dying from failure of the kidneys, uremia, a sleepy toxicity we tend to tell patients is no more unpleasant than taking a nap. How would we know that?

No matter his powers, he will not live long, the man with cancer of the pancreas. In the line of work in which I am training, most patients do not. What have they told you, I ask him, about your disease, about what happens next? But he will not look into his own future. I am afraid to, he admits. So I ask him what he hopes for now. This is a question we were trained to ask in an online module for orientation. It seems almost mean. I would not have come up with it on my own. The man has thin arms, a bony chest, wasted temples sunk into his cheek-bones. His bedbound state we sum up in two words: *poor reserve*. Cancer patients' rate of survival is in inverse proportion to the care they have come to require from others. Health is autonomy. This man cannot walk, cannot lift his hands to eat. I can see into his future: he will suffer a lot, and then he will die. I want only one thing, he tells me, but I already know what it is. He wants to live forever.

In the Beginning

We have one year to learn to care for the dying, one year and then the rest of our lives. All of the fellows are doctors, mostly young, fresh from residency, so we are a cohort trained all or mostly in the plague years. I was far enough from the city through the early surge that I did not, say, load bodies into refrigerated trucks, but a lot of the others were right here in the thick of it. They will not tell you what they saw, but they will tell you how they slept at night, or didn't, mostly drinking strong drinks and watching traumatic documentaries, videos of unwanted dogs scheduled to be euthanized or North Korean escapees recounting the murders of their families. When we start talking like this, reminiscing, we all start laughing at nothing; we laugh until we are short of breath and then for a long time no one says anything.

In orientation, all of the lectures are given on-line. A summer surge has made conference rooms once again untenable. You come to miss them, the bare walls and empty bookcases, the containment, the pleasant blankness of paneling. Medical libraries do not contain books. The science so quickly re-writes itself. On the screen the squares are crowded with faces, potted plants, trespassing cats. I watch from bed. As a group we are mostly white, mostly women, consistent with the demographics of the field, which is starkly white and has two women physicians for every one man. The gender skew re-lates to deep human traditions in the work of care, I guess, and the whiteness may be due to pallia-tive care's proximity to euthanasia. It pays poorly, too, on the spectrum of doctor money, like most caring or preventive fields with few procedures to bill for.

I rescued some books once from a liquidating medical library. *Human Diseases in Color,* a book of frightening medical photography, and *Dictionary of Symbols,* which must have been acquired in a time before Thorazine, when Jung was still relevant to the practice of psychiatry. The first few entries are

Abandonment
Ablution
Abracadabra
Abyss

The text beneath *abyss* is focused on the location of the abyss as it varies by culture: inside of mountains, at the bottoms of seas and lakes, over the horizon, or somewhere out in space. According to this dictionary, the abyss symbolizes not the unknown but the inferior. *Abracadabra,* it says, comes from the Hebrew, meaning hurl your thunderbolt even unto death.

One of the orientation lectures, after opioid conversions and remedies for constipation, is on talking points, branding, an early introduction to the field's bad rap. The host is center screen, upbeat, in a statement necklace of large colorful beads. She admits right away: I used to work in pharma, so I know how to spin! The trouble, she says, is all this talk about dying. The public does not want to hear about death.

Lead with life, she says, lead with what you have to offer. The cornerstone of her agenda is to demote the most common promotional images for hospice: a sunset viewed through parting clouds; a close-up of two white hands; an old hand atop a younger one, meaningfully clasped. She exclaims, over a slide of such an image: Enough with the hands!

In these early weeks, I am sent on home visits, cataloging homebound strangers' homes, while some of the cohort are sent to the clinic and some have already started in the hospital. The year is all laid out in advance. We will meet the dying in all of the settings we may later work in: the home, the clinic, the nursing home, the hospital. And we also see people who are not dying or are no nearer to death, as far as they know, than we are but who have curable cancers or chronic illnesses of other kinds and benefit in small and large ways from our wisdom in navigating health-care systems and dosing potent opioids.

Treating pain is the bulk of our work. By the time we are consulted in the hospital, the teams have reached the edge of their comfort—naproxen, acetaminophen, the almost useless pill for scorching nerve pain called gabapentin. We are trained to be comfortable with the stronger stuff: morphine, hydromorphone, fentanyl. We assess the risk that patients will use these drugs incorrectly, recreationally, and we dose them in ways that neither lead to euphoria nor hasten death. We are expert too in the other noises of the failing body: shortness of breath, nausea, constipation, insomnia. None of this is easy to be rid of. Bear with me, I tell the patients, if I get it wrong the first time. The patients we meet are in all phases of illness: newly diagnosed and still in shock or further along, beginning to build the illness into how they live, beginning to live against it, to refuse it, or starting to take it as a part of who they are. Even so, or perhaps because they live in such acute time, they will not forgive you for one drug-induced psychosis, for one unsuppressed projectile vomit, for the twitch of a mild morphine toxicity. Some, of course, turn down the drugs entirely, even when the pain is excruciating. I know what you are trying to do, they say, and they look you down with a hard, knowing look.

The best part, though, is the work we do in words. The palliative specialist serves as a sort of illness interpreter, bringing the jargon of clinical medicine into the life and language of the patient who is living the experience. We hold meetings between the patients and their doctors or, more often, between the families of the patients and the doctors, the families of patients who are too ill to speak for themselves. We hold these meetings at moments when the frame has shifted, when the assumed aim of medical intervention, the perpetual life of the body, has dissolved as a likelihood. These moments arise subjectively; some new day comes, or some new team, fresh sets of fresh eyes to take in the big picture. Often the task the other doctors need our help with is breaking bad news. They present the case, the impasse, with their gazes set centered, no eye contact: This is our fifty-four-year-old man with refractory lymphoma intubated for acute hypoxic respiratory failure. They get deep into the medical minutiae. We are trained to take their huge impartial confessions and render them in fewer words, a one-sentence summary that includes the primary medical update and the effect it has on the patient's immediate future. For example: Your father's cardiac arrest has led to the failure of his brain, lungs, liver, and kidneys, and for this reason we are afraid he will not live to leave the hospital.

The conflicts emerge in the words used around the families. They are *reasonable,* which comes in degrees, from *somewhat* to, in the best-case scenario, *very.* The families are reasonable to the extent that they share the perspective of the doctors. Predictable trajectories come with families who are *religious, hopeful,* and, most damning, *difficult.* There are other tells in the language. The word *unfortunately* is placed most often before a grim diagnosis—unfortunately with newly diagnosed lung cancer with metastasis to brain—but can itself metastasize to other descriptors: the family unfortunately hopeful; the patient unfortunately awake. And it is true most major religions have a say about decisions at the end of life, like in Orthodox Judaism, where life is breath, meaning no one comes off the ventilator. In the conference room, our team directs the seating. Although these meetings occur most often around long tables, you never want to sit oppositionally, with the family all on one side and the doctors on the other.

The trouble that the other doctors have is not a

lack of gentleness. Well, not only that. More often what they cannot do is tell the truth. They pack death up in so much misdirection, talk about the success or failure rate of this or that procedure or treatment, when the truth is the patient will be dead soon no matter what we come up with to do in the interim. That's the part they need a specialist to say. The families often cannot accept this in the moment, but still, it is good for them to know. You cannot know that, they often say, but we can, we do. You are not God, they will say if they believe in one. It is true, we do not have a crystal ball. That is what the doctors say quite often in response to an appeal to the deities, a stock phrase that equates religion with magic.

After breaking the news, the palliative specialist is trained to elicit the patient's values. We ask what matters most to them, or, if that does not land, we might ask what kinds of activities they formerly enjoyed. Some families can reliably play along in this effort, commit to the notion that we can make life-or-death decisions based on a person's likes and dislikes, on hobbies. A friend to everyone, he never wanted to be alone, he never wanted to be a burden.

A very private person. He hated doctors, no offense. Life or death, but it's always death. Maybe we should say, Now or later.

On the home visits, we are not always visiting basements. One patient on the Upper West Side, a very old man, has art all over his walls. He ushers us into the dining room. Mahogany, he says with a knock as we sit down at the long table. In addition to learning about his life and health, we ask him some questions regarding his possibly imminent dying. I haven't thought of it, he says. He is more than ninety years old. Honestly, though, he says, now that you bring it up, it scares me shitless, dying. Tell me more, I want to ask but the doctor I am working with has asked me not to speak. They go over his skills of daily living, his means of managing his complex regimen of medications. He has a wife and a nurse who do the legwork. Under his formal manner and eloquent speech, we find a man who cannot say what he ate today for breakfast. In the end, he shows us through the rooms, the walls all galleried. All French, he says, les Fauves. He has sketches by Matisse, Manguin, Derain. A still life in oil over a deceased fireplace. Cézanne, he says with a wave of his arm. Fruit, apples maybe, scattered on a white cloth, a teacup with the rim distorted into a swollen oblong. I have never seen or even imagined such things hanging in a person's home. The man appears bored. He herds us toward the door.

Another patient, in one of those brutal high-rises that top Central Park, survived the Khmer Rouge. The walls of her sickroom are covered in photographs of her as a nurse in Cambodia, older in a park surrounded by children. Her family is beautiful and she is beautiful, in her ninth decade, her hair still naturally brown. Her son at bedside looks twenty years younger than the age he must be. Who is he, the doctor I travel with asks, pointing to the son. What is his name? Him, she says. I've never seen him before in my life.

How she jokes, says the son.

The art collector settles on a full code. If I get sick, he says, do everything you can to keep me alive. So long as I am, you know, compos mentis. But he is not compos mentis now.

So we run to hospitals and clinics all over town. The teams consult us for refractory pain or nausea or suffering—the patients' or their own. Sometimes

19

they call us when they feel a patient needs to die, has no other alternative, needs to go ahead and get on with it. The patients' locations appear in the chart for as long as their bodies remain in the morgue. For unclear reasons, some stay down there for months. It breaks the heart. How we relate to one another, the dozen or so fellows, shows residue from the years we spent in competition with our various cohorts, climbing over each other for honors, awards, and prestigious postdoctoral training. Now that the main skill is communication, morning rounds can be a pageant in narrative, patient observations or recounted confessions elicited with this or that fellow's superior charms. He didn't tell you, a coy surprise, about his mother, when he was young, how she languished with cervical cancer? There was no use attempting, for example, to demonstrate the use of a comfortable silence. Someone would always jump in with another letter of the empathy acronym. One fellow, a future dual-certified colonoscopist, says one morning to me: When I saw your CV, I thought I would hate you!

A sculpture in the lobby of the main hospital depicts a shirtless, muscular doctor holding back

Death, his right hand on the heel of the Grim Reaper's scythe. In his left hand, he grasps a rod with two wings on its top and two snakes wound around it—it is the caduceus, the staff of the Greek god Hermes. In America it came to represent medicine after a well-known publisher confused it with the wingless, single-snaked rod of Asclepius, god of healing and medicine. Aptly, perhaps, to its American usage, the caduceus represents business, commerce, and thieves.

Communication Training

If you ask people in this country directly, seventy percent of them will say they want to die at home. I don't know about that, says the transplant cardiologist. People just don't want to die, and they feel further from dying if they are not in the hospital. My job is not to disagree. Everyone close to me who ever died did it at home, all of a sudden, with no preamble except the events, the habits, of their whole lives leading up to that moment. This is only a small number of people, one, really, and until very recently, I knew no one well who was dead at all. When I wrote a story about my life, it started: This is a story in which no one dies. But there are no stories in which no one dies. If no one has died, the story has not ended.

To make patients and their families view our work in a favorable light, we are trained to describe it without words and phrases that may strike the listener as too aversively death-oriented and therefore unattractive. This list includes:

Hospice
End-of-Life
Life-Limiting
Advanced Illness
Terminal Illness
Dying
Death

The study was meant to figure out why so many lives end badly. But of all the things on offer, no one wants straight talk. We are trying to treat a condition we are not allowed to diagnose.

So many of the fellows are recently bereaved—whether this led to our choice of subspecialty or is just a symptom of our demographics is unclear. After all the years of school and medical school and residency, we are suddenly old enough for our parents to be dying. I read so many personal statements, the program director says, describing fresh and terrible loss. I worry, she says. I think how awful this experience will be for you. This training, she means. The tools we are offered, casually, to cope are mainly in a psychoanalytic mode: This is about your family system and your childhood, the way you feel about the suffering of others, which you should recognize quickly and quickly conceal.

While I am still in school, my father often calls late at night to tell me he is dying. He provides no further detail or explanation; there is no prognosticating specialist of his whom I can call. He has been drinking, he is erratic, talking himself into rage. I learn to laugh at these terminal laments, finding no other recourse, to make sounds like laughter until he shouts: Who do you think you're laughing at? There is not necessarily a default form for the father in the mind of a child, no hole in that shape that needs to be filled. A father never needs to be present—many fathers sense this and, having found the out, take it.

For example, my earliest, most embodied memories are all fatherless: crumbling house, withdrawn young mother with cigarette tanning in the yard beside a cracked plastic wading pool where I stand with a leaf stuck to my leg, my brother holding the hose. My brother and I, alone together, running wild on bicycles, hiding in the arms of trees, setting fire to piles of sticks, leaves, and trash. As a child, I assume quite naturally that what happens to me happens to everyone, more or less, that there is a looming man they are driven across town to be left with, that on the drive over they get sick to their stomachs, that their teeth float in their mouths where their spit pools as they dread that looming father. The world, at first, is merely granted. Of course, children quickly pick up a sense that we have done wrong just by showing up. Screaming, needing clothing, becoming ill, putting an end to hopes and dreams our parents were not finished with. The children's needs, however, their burdens and their sense of themselves as a burden, are only necessarily embodied for the mother, in her presence. The father is notional. The father is a ghost.

Once, on a cross-country train, I run into my father. He is headed to Omaha for work, and I am on my way to see a friend in Denver. I am afraid enough of flying to often spend days on trains, to learn their names: the Lake Shore Limited, the Sunset Limited, the Empire Builder. This is the California Zephyr. He is with a crew of linemen he steers us away from. Cornpone is what he calls them, a word I do not know and look up later: those who have certain rural, unsophisticated particularities. I have not seen him for what has come to amount to several years. I do not go home, and he does not come to see me even when directly invited, even for the day that Eli and I are married. Although our meeting on a train in this way is remarkable, he does not remark upon it. I defer to his tone and affect. What we do in our seats, this rare shared proximity, is look out the window. He points out along the tracks the marks on all the trees, a few feet up, residual from a recent flood, and tells me in some detail how the ground is too hard now to soak up the rain, which falls harder and more often than it used to. Sudden deluges send huge crests outward down the river, surging over aging levees and dams. The kinds of floods we used to call catastrophic, he says, now happen every year, turning farms that were once floodplains into sheds and silos rising out of flat black water.

My father's father must have been a farmer, but he rarely shares his personal history. Great men, he says, talk about ideas, but his ideology evades me as well. I certainly never thought of him as an environmentalist. I thought of him as a spectacle, some sort of latent monster. I would bring friends out to his house when I was a teenager to use the canoes and show them this man, can you believe it? That he was as bizarre and smart and fearsome as I had told them. But they all had fathers; they were not impressed. Later, when he is dead, men will come to the funeral and tell me what a force he was for the union amid jokes about him getting so drunk, he threw the keys to his boat into the lake—from the boat into the middle of the lake—and someone interjects tearfully: All that aside, he really cared about the workers. And I will look at the box, which by then will be closed, and realize I do not know who any of them are talking about. He talks about the floods for maybe half an hour, then opens a newspaper and reads until Nebraska. Before the silence, one thing I ask him is if he is happy. He has just gone through another divorce, but he has his house at the lake, the cars, the boat, all his antique model planes and handguns. He says, What the hell kind of question is that? Who asks a person something like that?

27

He never lived in a house with us, but still he raised my brother and me with a sense of ourselves as burdens or obstacles, a sense that I, at least, never quite got over. He taught us at a young age the math of payroll deductions for child support: a quarter of his income on account of my brother and another five percent for each subsequent child, of which there was only me. And I knew that he had dropped out of a graduate program in history, a master's degree, something that once seemed grand to me and mysterious, when we were young, and I assumed this loss was also caused by us children. But later he tells us that when I was quite young, an infant, and he and our mother were already separated, he got quite drunk and took a short ride in a fast car he had just bought and hit a row of parked cars so hard that his car was wedged entirely beneath the first one he hit, completely creamed, as he put it, flattened with him inside. He recounts his extraction, seeming to love the phrase *jaws of life*. He has photographs from the scene, which he keeps in a briefcase under his bed, clippings from the front page of the town paper. And he was in intensive care for months after, for facial fractures and brain bleeding, though his torso, his limbs, were unharmed. He lived in a morphine fugue state until he was well enough to walk, and then he checked out against medical advice. I know now a lot about traumatic brain injuries, the frontal lobe and what it is good for: impulse control, social function, planning, and insight. So I sometimes wonder about the father I might have had if the accident had never happened or how my life would be different if he had died.

There is a lesson to be learned here, I think, and then live only in cities where nobody drives.

Alignment

The families rarely know what the patients would have wanted. A constant reminder of the firm boundaries between the everyday world and the hospital. The outbreak seemed to change this only a little, only for a short while, when the public got interested suddenly by necessity in ventilators. When we had to figure out how to assign them, in case we ran out, the ethics committee crafted triage guidelines that were based on a patient's remaining years of quality life, on likelihood of overall survival. But when we ask people who do not work in the hospital what they think matters most, they ask about the cost: Could we see the bill, at least an estimate, before we choose to go on a ventilator?

This is my first day in the clinic where I will

work one afternoon a week for a year, seeing the people with serious illness in their own clothes, in their own lives, outside the confines of the hospital. Today's first patient, I have been warned, is a splitter. A splitter is a patient who likes some people, but she doesn't like you. She, but they are always women. In the hospital, only some kinds of cognitive dissonance are pathologized. The inference is that she has a disorder of personality, that she oscillates meaninglessly between extreme assessments of the value of others. Fine. I tend to fall on splitters' good sides, a tendency that points to something I know is wrong with my character: I allow too much. The patient, her voice, gets me right away, although I can't say why until it comes to light that she grew up in the plains states, one west of the one I grew up in. She reminds me of those hometown people. A kindness that is tonal, not semantic, the voice of a people who will eat you alive. When she enters the room, it fills at once with a strange and wonderful smell—frankincense, I soon find out, and balsam fir from the topical oils she is using to treat her cancer. A tumor the size of a dove nests in her left lung.

I worked with an attending in residency who

is also a famous skeptic. He is an activist against homeopathy. I didn't tell him about my doubts about rationalism as a project. But I did ask: Isn't it, some of it, harmless? I had recently attempted to use lavender oil to treat agitation in the neuroscience ICU. Harmless? He made a serious face. It is always dangerous, he told me, to teach patients that magic is real.

Mindfulness, at least, has the full backing of science. We are all encouraged to practice it by our program administration. There are signs that the fellows are running low on resilience. I am a good sport, good enough to get an app on my phone that sends intermittent messages, inspirational or cryptic, sometimes vaguely like a threat. One day a message reads: YOU ARE THE WORLD'S LEADING EXPERT ON BEING THE SAME PERSON YOU WERE YESTERDAY. The app reminds me to breathe, to move purposefully, to recall that this very moment is the only one I have. Whatever I am doing, it isn't working. Where I am is trapped in a stalled subway train somewhere on the long stretch of track between where I live and everything that matters. FEELING STUCK? the phone asks. TRY THIS EXERCISE TO CENTER YOURSELF.

Now on the train, it is the convention to put more space between yourself and others, to leave alternate seats empty for as long as is reasonable. Masks are commonplace but not universal. I am grateful for mine as the car fills up with smoke: on the opposite end, someone has lit a cigarette. A woman to the left of me stacks and unstacks a number of ceramic plates she has padded with the two legs of a single pair of pants. She keeps rearranging, realigning the plates on her lap, dropping the plates, upsetting the man next to her, who appears fatigued with trying to catch them. The woman on my other side has an eye full of blood, a subconjunctival hemorrhage. It is benign but still unsettling. I see the blood and then look down at the book she is reading. The title is *Reclaim Your Power!* On the page I can see over her arm a man's silhouette surrounded by arrows or vectors in the shape of a triangle standing on a time-line with just one point. The point is labeled NOW.

During the week, Eli goes back out to the sub-urbs, where he still works, and the reverse commute is long enough that many nights he stays out there with a friend, a divorced anesthesiologist he knows from the hospital. This friend has a finished shed in his yard with no insulation but wired for electricity, a kind of low-end guesthouse. One night he invites Eli into the main house and serves him chana masala and asks if he is interested in a romantic relationship. The anesthesiologist is not gay, but Eli's presence, their constant contact, has generated in him a measure of ardor he says he has never before felt in his life. Given that Eli works as a religious professional, it is odd that no small number of his friends and acquaintances, especially through work, and even people who know us both, who know me socially and are not unfriendly toward me, will pull him aside or keep him late in the office to profess their love for him. Most surprising, to me, at least, is these admirers always assume they are acknowledging a shared burden and, having boldly revealed it, now need only to transcend love's obstacles—the chief of which is, in every case, me.

In part I understand. I fell for Eli in the same way, fast, in or near the moment I met him, struck like that, acute and viral. He still likes to hear me recount those early days, mostly just us being hungry and walking around the city and being poor together. He had told me right away it would never work out. How he laughed at the wedding, as if he could not believe what I had gotten him into. Now, to myself, on sleepless nights, I play it back from the start, not from my own perspective but from some outside place, and I can see all the red flags, the cracks in the foundation, the pathologies already in place. I do not know if this trouble is specific to us, a bad match, or if perhaps these are problems that everyone has: one partner wanting, for instance, to purchase a four-hundred-dollar lamp, and the other wanting to strip down to nothing and step away from his clothes and step away from his home and set his house on fire.

At the bedside, expressions of love are not frequent or grand, not at all the way they play out on TV medical dramas. There are some late-life weddings, usually unions of long-standing couples who put it off until one party began to succumb to serious illness. It is unclear to me if these weddings offer any financial benefit to the newlywed survivor or if they serve primarily to worsen the paperwork. For example, the next of kin is responsible for the disposition of remains and has to choose whether or not the body will be autopsied. If you are legally married, no matter how separated or estranged, no matter the years since you last met or made contact, this spouse has to be found and asked for consent. Autopsies are seldom performed as it is. The trouble this causes relates to the lack of certainty in discerning cause of death. Doctors, so prized for their rightness, are wrong regarding cause of death one time out of three. Without autopsy, there is no forum to offer this fact, specifically, as feedback.

The hospital weddings are bleak in every case, the minister often brought in on a tablet, the vows with an echo, a lag. Till death do us part does not mean much around here. Often they just leave it out. The long-married hospice patients show the most remorse. Usually this presents as a low-grade detachment but sometimes it expresses as fulminant rage. One man tells me, more than twice: I hate my wife, and she knows why. And I will wonder why forever. Something I ask when I just want to hear patients speak, tell a story, in order to assess their cognitive status or language capacity, is how they met their spouses or partners. And more and more, they say apps or online, but sometimes, with the old folks, you get a good one: We met at a dinner in the Temple of Dendur. We met at a high-school dance. We met at a smoking-cessation group run by the American Red Cross. And you quit? They did—neither ever smoked again. There is always something else to die from. So that is what I asked that dying husband. Oh, her, fuck her, he says. The biggest mistake of my life. A forty-year mistake.

Sometimes the trouble seems to be, to Eli, that I cannot prove I love him in particular. It is true, for example, that I cannot go to sleep alone in the dark. When I try, I invariably become seized with terror, I go apneic and startle, unnamed and shapeless shapes in darkness spiral in my visual field, and so I require company to sleep, and—it is true—no company in particular. Even a dog works, or works halfway, or more than halfway, proportional to the alertness of the dog, though I learned this well into the marriage.

The splitter is back. This is clinic again. She is waiting for a biopsy that keeps getting bumped. I see her weekly and she gives me the same speech, recounting the hells she has lived through by allowing herself to be subjected to Western medicine. She describes a surgeon's superficial charm, the way he overpowered her, tricked her into going under the knife. She attributes to this surgery a long-standing pain in her back and the fact that she never enjoyed smoking again. I listen with two ears, two minds, one for what is real and one for what is true. She ends up feeling that we are aligned. And one day, when it's just her and me, she starts to share her thoughts about the virus, the vaccine. You don't have to wear that, she says about my mask, we both know they don't do anything. And she names some radio-talk-show host, a real man of science, she calls him, and she shares that although she is a full code, she'd never want to go on a ventilator, because that is another progressive scam, to keep you sick and charge you for it. I understand the appeal of conspiracy, that someone, anyone, is controlling all of this.

I did not mean to become an absolute relativist. A response, perhaps, to the staunchly objectivist doctors who trained me. I never understood why Heisenberg and all those men in the early twentieth century didn't have a broader philosophical impact on the sciences. The world is unknowable—that is a fact. Then I hear the man who was my boss, the doctor in charge of my residency, telling me with little amusement: Some things are just true. Like what, I ask. Like levetiracetam treats epilepsy. Levetiracetam is the most commonly prescribed anti-seizure medication in the world. But there is a story there too, a soft spot—the story that epilepsy is a disease. The place where uncertainty disturbs me most, though, is in the home, in the marriage. I spent a long time longing for Eli when we were first together, when for months and months he worked quite hard to keep me at a remove. During this time I would lie in bed at night most nights and remember everything I could about every good moment that had already happened: a certain embrace, his face in some kind of light. I would try to believe it was enough.

The splitter comes to love me, finds her way to calling me by my first name, and the things she says get worse and worse the more I come to see her. It isn't just the vaccine stuff. In the safe space I make for her, she is a 9/11 truther, a chemtrail believer, says all modern wars are based on lies. Even the Second World War, she says, smiling. But I'm not supposed to talk about that. And then I start to dread seeing her or even put it off. No time, I tell myself, and then feel guilty about it. I feel, too, gradually, a strange sensation that a trap has closed over me, an old trap. I should have known better.

The trouble is, not all of what she believes is untrue. There is fluoride in the water, genetic interventions bred into the plants. Microwaves were, it is true, designed as weapons of destruction. But to other facts—that the world is round, that men (mostly men) by actions or inaction have killed millions, left them in piles, in mass graves and trenches, that that has happened and will happen and is happening now—suddenly it is an option to just say: No. Not true, not real, not happening. That great evil is possible feels true, is a fact about the whole world that my body seems to know. But what if I were made differently? I think about the photographs I saw in middle school, the bodies in ditches, the piles of shoes. Where is the line between rejecting that feeling because you cannot stand it and rejecting the truth as truth? The whole body wants to get away from it.

I once saw a therapist for just a few sessions who believed you could use hypnosis to cure brain tumors. What a nourishing thought, that cancer killed only those ignorant of this practice or too weak of mind to get the job done. I had called Employee Health, the emergency line for trainees, after developing an invisible tremor, a condition I knew could not exist outside the realm of psychiatry. The trouble was that I could feel that inside I was shaking, though no movement was present to discern with the naked eye. I began to supplement myself with B vitamins in case this was how it felt to begin to have neuropathy. I worried, though not to the extent of seeing, say, a doctor, that my off-hours habits—something that was not quite anorexia meeting something that was not quite alcoholism—were depleting me of phosphorus, or thiamine, or some other agent that supported an inner sense of stability.

A few weeks after I start canceling the splitter's appointments, a man follows me off the train. It is my fault, in a way. I was looking, staring maybe, at his ankles, where he had tattooed NO FUN. One word on each. I was trying to imagine a reason for this, the life in which a person would think to have this phrase tattooed on his ankles and then do it, one word on each. And I saw him stand to get off at what I guessed was his stop, but he didn't get off. He waited for my stop and then followed me. And now, while I am afraid, what I feel most is guilty for suspecting this, or provoking it, or something. He touches my elbow on the street corner when we surface. He says, I just wanted to say hello. He says, Is that allowed? It is not, I tell him, no. No, he says as though telling himself, and then he walks away.

Even that therapist—it took me weeks to fire him. First I avoided any self-disclosures; I turned all of our talks onto him. I learned about his childhood, a failed adoption, his time in finance, brief work as a Baptist pastor. All I ever said was: Tell me more about that. So dismissing the man from the train so fast feels at first like an accomplishment. Then it comes to feel like something else.

I am afraid of the splitter, then, is maybe what I mean. Or afraid that aligning with her means something horrible about me, that I provoke this kind of thing, that I bring it upon myself. And I never want to see her again, I think, and then see her again at her next appointment. She has shown me something strange inside of me, a wound shaped like distrust and disgust and familiarity. We exaggerate the differences between ourselves and others; I think this must be true, so I am trying to believe it.

Visiting Hours

In a dream one night I am watching a horror movie set in a sprawling farmstead leased as a vacation rental. I am in the movie and viewing it simultaneously. I am with Eli, a younger version of him, startlingly handsome. I tell him I do not think we can enjoy the movie if, as it seems, we are in it. The constant threat of death will make it hard to relax. And what will happen if we die? Will we see the end? If so, from where will we be watching? From inside the movie, it is obvious that peril applies equally to everyone around, even the children, who have only bit parts in the scenes in which they appear. From inside, it is not obvious that the gratuitous deaths of even children, meaningless and awful and disconnected from the plot, will be prevented by producers or test-screening viewers who will find it innately unpalatable. There are no such restrictions you can see from the inside. The entire scenario is immediately unbearable in its terror, even though nothing is happening beyond the ominous soundtrack. But Eli and the others still want to explore the beautiful rural environs. It is the kind of place where you might have a high-end country wedding. Anyway, we die right away, in the first instance of violence, before the miasmic, supernatural premise even makes itself clear. But all of the dead remain present after the initial attack. We understand ourselves to be ghosts despite having the same opacity as the survivors.

Sarah, my brother's child, the one he has left with us, knows I am a doctor and holds some interest in this fact. She is afraid of her pediatrician, an austere stranger who sometimes causes pain. She seems to know about death but does not ask about it directly. For instance, in a children's song including the line *Perhaps she'll die,* Sarah adds after that the word *forever* in a blaring trombonish tone. When we first picked her up, we believed it would be for a week or two, a month at most, though looking back, I find it hard to believe that we really believed that. How generous, everyone says, meaning not of us, but of Eli. What kind of man would want to raise another man's child? The child's presence both balms and augments a commitment I had permanently deferred regarding our own children—that is, that we would have any. Sarah is five now, in kindergarten. She shows me, one day, beaming, her class photograph, three rows of children, some who look like toddlers and others who look as old as seven, having lost time locked down in their homes, sheltered from the virus.

There was a time when Eli thought he would become a priest. He enrolled, though that is not the word, in seminary, graduated, but was never ordained. His call, as it were, got disconnected. He left the process between the step called discernment and the one called supplication. Not to marry. This was High Church Protestantism, where priests can marry and, I believe, divorce. I still don't know why it happened, which is odd because I was there.

We did have all those essential premarital conversations. We agreed to have children, agreed not to try to be rich, agreed that we wanted our lives to be of some good to other people. He is an altruist, as real as they come; meanwhile, I have long known my life would not be good for me, so living for others gives me at least some reason to keep showing up. Bearing children—imagined as they were—does seem like part of a life that could reasonably be expected of me, a presumably fertile person in a woman's body. I put it off. I would meet them, children, sometimes at work in residency, see them sick and suffering in a way I couldn't stand to see. I have no aversion at all to seeing the worst of what you can do to an adult, but seeing the suffering of children destroys me. One time, rotating in pediatric emergency, I saw a child who was brought in having not woken up from a nap. Scans of the brain showed retinal hemorrhages and bilateral subdural hematomas, the signature injuries of nonaccidental trauma. And while I did suggest the correct medicine to stop the seizure he was suddenly having, I proceeded to leave the trauma bay, collapse in the hall, and vomit into a trash can. The greatest risk factor for abusing children, the attending says, is having been abused as a child.

Have you suffered enough? I wondered this about Eli when we met, when he told me how he wanted to live his life. I did not, at the time, want to give anything away. I would never have enough, I was sure of it then, sure that there was nothing I could ever earn or win or have that would change this fact about my life. But Eli was something else. We would show up places, meet there. Eat or drink? What kinds of things would he tell me? He saved my life, I think, by letting me love him. And once you save someone, you always will have done it. One night, in the beginning, he told me he could never have a wife or a family, anyone in his life, who would be harmed by or scold him for outrageous acts of charity. Imagine I come home from work, he said, having met someone who needed a car, and I would have to tell some wife I had given away ours?

You can see clearly now the problem with the lamp. And now of course Eli does have a car, a sort of wife, a sort of child. He has certain kinds of insurance and retirement accounts he doesn't know how to use or access. In the moment when we met, perhaps we both believed ourselves to be radical or capable of radical things, and now, having turned out to be enough like anyone, we are embarrassed for each other, for what we have been present for, the failures and compromises to which we have been witness.

One night, early on, we were walking through a neighborhood of stark concrete apartments, and we saw a Hasidic man walking just ahead of us suddenly collapse to the ground. Around that time I had been thinking a lot about falling and physical comedy, about the humor that is found in violence without consequence, that falling down is funny because that is what we do when we die. But this was not funny, although he was not dead. Yet I could not, did not, rush toward him. In my limited experience I seemed to know I was not supposed to touch him, and it was not clear to me if this was due to my gentilism or my apparent gender, but Eli ran straight to his side, assessed his vital well-being like a television paramedic. And I was in awe; in a way I was in love immediately with a way of being in the world that allowed one to rush toward need so unselfconsciously. Over time I would link his easiness in the world with his handsomeness, his whiteness, his masculinity. All of us go through our lives being treated like someone who looks the way we look. I have had a lot of privilege too. My privilege most often is to be left alone. We were taught in medical school that we are permitted to touch anyone, as the tasks of our work demand it, but I didn't know if Hasidic men had also been taught that.

So often I meet people when they are deeply ill, perhaps I could say very seriously ill, when they are tied down with straps, with endotracheal tubes in their mouths held in place with plastic braces that adhere to the cheeks and obscure most of the face. I am there in these cases to perform a task called palliative extubation. Once we remove all of the machines, we always tell the families death will take hours to short days, meaning as little as an hour or up to a few days—the days themselves are of the usual length, and, if anything, it seems that the days spent at vigil with the imminently dying tend to get a little long. In contrast to their bound-up and medicalized selves, their freed bodies, the faces in particular, are always shocking to me in their beauty. I tell this to one patient's wife when I go to get her—we put the families in a little conference room for the duration of the procedure of removing the breathing tube and while we settle the patients in, clean them up, titrate the sedatives. He looks beautiful, I say, not so much to move her as to let her know I am paying attention. He's always been easy on the eyes, she says. And later, over his body once he is dead, she shows me pictures on her phone of him when he was well, before he was eaten up by the cancer that grew in his stomach and then in his bones and his lungs. But in the photos she shows me, he is just some man. Now, I mean, he is beautiful.

When I think of his face after his death, it is not as an image with a referent in the world but rather as a way of relating to the world that has as its only referent this experience, the experience of watching him die, of having appeared there myself, with him, having been present. This presence displaces the ordinary filter the mind holds over the senses.

I meet a fellow in training in intensive care who hates the pictures the families bring and show or tape to the walls, vacation snapshots or wedding photos, the patients beaming and well in better times, enjoying the silence of their organs. If I see that they are really human, he says, I cannot be objective. I won't try to change your mind, I tell him, but there is no such thing as objective. Relying on what you decide to call pure reason means only that you leave your bias unexplored. That's fine, he says, his tone uninvested. My mind will never change on this. Imagine believing that, I mean about anything.

Enlighten the Dead

In the first version of the psychedelic revolution, all of the clinicians tried the drugs themselves. It is important, they thought, to know what it is that we are going to do to others. Elsewhere, though, surgeons do not undergo default appendectomies, psychiatrists don't test-drive electroconvulsive therapy. I did, once, trial an antipsychotic against my will. It made me feel only that I needed to tilt my head to the left, further and further, until it got so hard to hold I had to lay it down.

But I do try grief before my fellowship starts. In a dark month of the first pandemic winter, in the last leg of my residency training, my father wakes one morning and makes his bed and sits in his chair and dies. He is found days later with hand on chest, the small-town coroner notes, and the look of someone taken by surprise. My father was a man who once paid a thousand dollars to autopsy a cat he loved when it turned up dead in the yard. He was seized with an irrevocable notion that the neighbors had poisoned the cat vindictively. The autopsy revealed that the cat had indeed died from ingesting poison, though nothing in the body, the little bleeding guts and broken-down mucosa, could prove how the poison had come to be in there. It had to be assumed, and was accordingly documented, that the cat had poisoned itself by accident.

The first death I see, I mean the moment itself, while I am a fellow is an old man with no children, an artist of some midrange renown, with cancer at the end of a good long life. His death does not come out of the blue but on a timeline more expedited than he had dared to imagine.

He wants to go home, is all, but home is a small walk-up with narrow halls, narrow stairs, and he cannot walk and cannot breathe without high-flow nasal oxygen. I am sorry, I tell him—despite communication training, I still sometimes say this—and he says, Of course it cannot be your fault. It seems to me, though, that someone should apologize.

Between the time when he is last able to speak and the time that he is gone, there is an interval I will come to know well, what we call actively dying, though it is mainly and ideally a time of stillness, except almost always the body is working harder to breathe. As the blood pressure drops and the blood loses oxygen, the color of the skin changes from whatever it is to gray, and the lips turn a waxy off-white, and the breath becomes the only suggestion of the life now mostly gone, though it too has gone strange, become odd and mechanical, as if some kind of gasket mechanism was built into the chest, raising and lowering the sternum with effort, without rhythm, some mechanical relic from an old haunted house. This is what lasts hours to short days. When I see him last, he looks uncomfortable, though I am only guessing this based on his rate of respiration. Nothing else about him expresses anything that looks like a human experience. With the support of the attending, I dose him with a potent IV opioid, and while I watch to see the effect, I see his breathing stop and not start again. I watch his pulse in his neck for a long time. It fades so slowly it is hard to say when it stops. When you listen to the chest, what you hear is your own pulse coming faintly through the bell of the stethoscope. The eyes are where it is obvious. Pupils fixed, mid-position. Nothing else really looks like that.

One of the hospitals where we work is half empty, a renovation abandoned when funding was cut after the virus. You have to walk across an empty ward to find the skybridge that labyrinths toward the palliative-care office. The empty rooms have no beds and are seldom swept. The corners hold small tumbleweeds of human hair and hollow dead palmetto bugs. The main hospital bought it up, this community hospital, and tried, it seems, to liquidate it. The process misfired, and now the administration holds the building in a state of indecision. The emergency department, at least, is always full. On the way to work one day I see a man on the subway platform splayed out in such a way that I have to step over him. Because of his presence, his physical imposition on my path, I do ask at least if he is all right. Do you need help, I ask. I am afraid he will say yes. No, no, he says, or seems to say. To make toothlessness and its impediment to speech less uncouth, we use the term *edentulous*. But later that day, rushing to an urgent consult to clarify the treatment goals of a woman hemorrhaging into her brain stem, I pass him being rolled in on a stretcher, appearing unconscious, and think to myself: Continuity.

No one prepares you for this, says the wife of that first man I watch die. We have been trying to get her to visit for days, firing warning shots, the old guard calls it: His breathing is quite shallow, time is getting short. But she does not show up.

A ringing phone has always sounded like disaster to me. This time too. What am I doing? When Sarah is in bed, Eli and I will sit and watch the same old television over and over, surrealist murder mysteries. Dad is dead, my brother says when I pick up. I must express some terse disbelief, ask what, how, or why. It seems so out of sequence. It is unwarranted. I mean, without warning. Soon I ask why my brother decided to say it so abruptly. I considered saying he is gone, my brother says, but I was afraid you would say, Gone where?

He does not know what happened. He sounds far off or stoned, as he often does, and despite my training I cannot say if it is cannabis or cough syrup or methadone. He is supposed to be in Utah somewhere, but I do not ask. I try not to think about

Sarah being alone with him in the time before she came to us. What do you think her life was like, the psychologist asks. Surely not always frightening, not always dangerous. All I can imagine, besides varied cusps of violent harm, is the two of them watching television, her beside him, close but not touching, staying up late into the night, watching nature documentaries. I imagine them watching one I have seen, one about the ocean and a haze of poison brine in the depths of the Pacific where the deep-sea eels writhe in the dark water. He was in the easy chair, my brother tells me. It had been a couple of days. There was a gun on the table, and a pile of money, a few hundred dollars cash. The cat was crying at the door so loud the neighbors heard and found him. Drugs, I ask, though our father did not do drugs. No, he says, and no signs he, well, did it himself.

Do I ask my brother to leave rehab against medical advice and drive across the country in a rental car in a surging plague to meet me in the shit town where we grew up to handle things, to get dressed up and bury our father? He would want you there, I say. More than me, I mean. And he knows it is true, and still he does not come.

A Minor Celebrity

It is fall all at once. The summers have been hot and long for years, ending abruptly in months of freezing rain, but this year is the miracle. The first leaves to turn are the poison ivy in the woods, retreating from the edges of the footpaths, belying some small sense of safety. Eli, on his weekends home from work, takes a sudden and consuming interest in bicycles and is gone suddenly, constantly, off riding a bicycle or going to other boroughs to street fairs to see bicycles in great lineups on the street. The front hall becomes crowded with bicycles we bend ourselves sideways to get around.

That first death is one of few I retain with any specificity. Before long they come so quickly, I cannot possibly register them all with the same sense of weight. In one case I care for an elderly film actress. She has become, somehow, in her late life, married to her agent, a well-tended man several decades her junior. It is not clear at the time what the actress has for cognitive capacity. The partner shields her from our attention as if we are overeager members of the press. He answers for her, deflects our questions about dyspnea and pain as if we wish to own or publish her, to make her frailty publicly known, rather than to titrate her standing hydromorphone. The tablet form of heroin, I hear someone call it, though we give plenty intravenously as well. This is what I gave the first man right before I watched him die.

Should I wonder if I killed him? We are all a small part of larger causes and conditions; this is why legality requires that soft-focused notion of intent. In residency I also become party to some deaths in ways that feel a little too direct. We give an IV drug to dissolve the blood clots that cause stroke, and the first and second time I give it—because of the risks, the nurses actually make us push it ourselves—both patients bleed massively into their strokes and die. The sensation of proximity to volitional harm, harm unto death, is both heavy and surprisingly abstract.

When I turn to my mentors, they give knowing shrugs and say only: Maybe it was for the best.

I don't know much about the actress, though I recognize her name. She had been involved in some derailing scandal in the seventies and never quite came back, though her clout still earned her a room in the VIP unit, what administrators call the amenities suite. Regarding her feeding tube, which was surgically implanted in her abdomen, the agent admits: I talked her into it! It really is quite obvious he cannot let her go. His whole manner, his eyes and his face and his body, speaks of a deep and easy love for the actress, and it is so easy to see and admire, coming straight from his heart without the obscuring veils of coping with logistics or mentioning the costs of it all, the way the poor and obscure always have to, worry for the bills or the time off work, the burdens of tending to logistics even at such tense and unfrivolous times. The agent is not afflicted in this way; he does not require a voucher to pay for his parking. But he does have regrets. Often when families lament this or that late-game decision, I assure them with a straight face that they have done nothing wrong or even that they have made the right choice entirely. Right enough, I say only to myself. I no longer believe, at least not usually, that most of the choices we make matter at all. After watching clips of her old films, learning the lines of the face she used to have, I come to feel something like reverence when I see the actress in bed. She is so small, so diminished, you almost cannot see it, but when you do, you see all at once all the ages of her face, so to see her now is to have aged with her. You feel a part of her history, and everyone here is suddenly a part of something larger, something with as much impact as a major motion picture. But she dies the same as anyone.

Another early one that sticks: a woman with aggressive cancer in her throat. Now it is in her right vocal cord. As it grows, she will struggle to eat, then she will struggle to breathe. Already she chokes on her food if she is not careful. Last night she choked with her son in the room. I panicked, the son says. He is somehow apologizing to me. This is in the hall, around a bend, in the unit that wraps like a U around a bank of desks, the rooms with glass walls that bend and fold away quickly in emergencies. She has never seen me cry like this in my life. In the room alone with the mother, I lean in with my stethoscope. I got to tell you something, she tells me. Let me listen, I say. To her body, I mean. I hear her voice through the bell, filling the airy space in her chest. God told me to tell you this, she says. That there is something you need to know, something you are wrong about. What's that, I ask. The possibilities are endless. He says you think you got here on your own.

But here is a place I want to get out of. I start to spend weekends off at a place upstate I find online, looking for a cheap retreat. A monastery where most of the monks, the monks and nuns, speak only Vietnamese. The bunks are barren, says an online review, but the cooking is excellent. I do not know if what I wanted was a break from death or from my family. The place feels correct immediately; I am relieved, and among the weird crowd of tourist visitors I feel correctly anonymous. The first man who speaks after the first meditation, after the little talk for visitors on the rules of the place from a nun called Sister Empathy, announces that he and his family have come to cope with a recent loss. Our son, he says, her brother. He gestures toward a girl

of maybe fifteen. We know the teachings on imper-
manence, he says, but we have a lot of questions.

The place is split in two by a country road. The
bigger half is for the men, the monks and the male
visitors. The women and the families stay with the
nuns. I am assigned to a bunk bed in the hall of a
small bungalow. The woman with whom I share it is
asleep when I arrive and sleeps through orientation.
Afterward I find her reading in bed using a small
lamp she wears on an elastic headband. She says she
is a professor, a sociologist of mass communication.
I come here to recharge, she says. She snores as well,
both a comfort and a bother through the first night,
which is otherwise shocking in the thickness of its
silence. I keep thinking of the dead son. In the orientation circle we are all asked why we have come.
After the father shares, a tall woman with a low
voice says she is here to prepare for some suffering
about to befall her. This piques my interest too. She
looks so well. Perhaps she has just been diagnosed
with cancer or is awaiting major surgery. It is hard to
imagine what other suffering one could anticipate so
punctually. Later in the night I see her with tea in the
common area. I sit down and ask her what she sees

63

coming. Oh, she says. A punk-rock band is about to release some songs about me. She shares that she has recently been diagnosed with schizoaffective disorder—psychosis with dysregulated mood not otherwise meeting the criteria for schizophrenia.

What kind of psychosis, I ask her. I am not sure whether this is a generous or an invasive question, but she does not seem bothered. I am trying not to be afraid of her, since she will be sleeping so near to me. But I am afraid anyway. The nuns keep a large vat near the sink in the common room labeled STRONG ACID, evoking thoughts of mass suicide by caustic ingestion. Delusions of reference, the woman tells me. Like hearing a line from a radio ad and you know it is meant only for you. Sounds frightening, I offer. No, she says. It is wonderful. On my turn in the circle, I say I am taking a break from work.

Sometimes I see plainly that the mind is only noise, and I find a way to live mostly underneath the din. I can spend a few days wandering around this way, euphoric, a happy ghost. With no insides to tend to, I am an excellent physician. In clinic I care for a woman who is dying from insidious unstoppable paralysis. She lives in an electric wheelchair. In the short time I have known her, she has lost the use of her one good hand. Now if she eats, it is her son who raises the fork to her mouth. We make a point to record her voice reading children's books aloud while she still can speak, though her children are grown and she does not have grandchildren. This is called a legacy project. I fear but do not mention that the ones she might one day have would not want to hear a dead woman reading them a story. We are always telling children what has weight and meaning. No matter what we say, though, they do not believe it. What they get from us, they get from exposure, not instruction. Sarah says to herself, failing to tie her shoe: Why am I the worst? Why am I the worst child? Variations on self-talk she must have learned from me.

A few months in, I have seen the end come for so many people, all ages, all ethnicities, from all social strata, that when I walk down the street I can look at most of the people and have a reasonable sense of what they would look like dead or dying. Maybe this sounds as if it would cause some kind of despair, but it does not. One morning, it is the day after daylight saving starts, and I feel I have been pulled from death when my alarm goes off. I look around on the train, face the faces there, and recognize as smoothly as the surface of the seats, the words of the ads, that all of us will die, and that in a sense of time as a folded cloth, with layers of past and future smoothed on top of one another, brushed flat with the unseen hand of—of whom? That all of us are dead already.

A Different Place

The monastery is a kind of commune, clusters of worn structures for small rooms and bunks and a few larger halls for meditation and eating. The rest is narrow paths through old woods with worn stone in many of the walking places, overgrown with soft moss and lichen, the only green in the winter woods. Enjoy the nature, says Sister Empathy, but never walk alone. There are bears. I do take to the woods often and alone but do not go far before a kind of fear grips me. The arrival of the fear is not unwelcome, though. It shows me that for a moment, the fear was gone. The rest of the day is just sitting and standing, sitting again, as one monk or another leads a talk on attention. You have heard this before, says the teaching monk, but I am sharing my aspect.

At the beginners' session that opens each weekend, Brother Emptiness asks for our dharma. A blond man with a blond beard says he has been having a problem with insight. I just can't seem to hold on to it. He wants to know if the sangha has any tips. But someone from the back row has a more pressing question. It is that father from before. He says, What I am wondering is—what is the purpose of living? There is a small amount of laughter in response to this, but it is not a joke. Brother Emptiness speaks slowly. He was a child in Vietnam during the war, and then he was a refugee. He grew up, he got a job in finance, he worked. It was in retirement, he says, that I got more—he pauses, gestures at his robes— existential. The point somehow is that we all have to find a path. I liked your question, I tell the father after, in the common room. My son, he says, started asking that question when he was seven. What did you tell him? Nothing, says the father. I was incapable. I have a reasonable guess that the son has died by suicide, from the suddenness, the demographic. Still, I ask. The father places a hand around his own throat and then tightens his grip.

It is almost winter solstice and I am working

on the palliative-care unit. It is like an ICU except everybody dies. Everybody, nearly everybody. It is cold and dark in the morning and it is dark at night when we leave. When I get in, the nurse practitioner says, Good morning, Doctor, leaning into the title as if making fun of me. Then she says who died overnight. Some nights, it is no one; some nights up to five. Good, good, I sometimes say—the only time it isn't at least kind of good is when the patient's stay with us was meant to be only a brief segue to a different disposition, home, say, and the suddenness of the expected end amounts to a surprise. The NP and I sit side by side in a very small office, closet-size, with no windows, no art, white walls covered in corkboard with papers pinned everywhere. Instructions for procedures I just ask the NP how to do anyway: how to call the medical examiner, how to fend off the eye bank. It is like riding in a car together, that is the proximity. She is driving.

We come to feel at odds with the organ-procurement people, though the virtue of their mission is obvious. The trouble is that we grow protective of our patients in death, protective of these final moments, and the organ people carry a different set of interests. By law we must call them whenever a patient is on the way out. If they accept the patient as a candidate for donation, the case shifts away from our quiet plans and toward aggressive measures to preserve the organs of interest. Depending on the plan for harvest, the patient may be transferred to a different unit or to the ICU. From the perspective of justice, of resource allocation, of doing the most good for the most people, it is wrong of us to want our patients left alone. It is just a feeling we come to harbor, that the person in front of us is the most important person in the world. I say *we* but this might be my own problem. The NP at least shares my aversion to the eye bank. In order to take the cornea, the transplant people perform a bedside enucleation. They take it all, the whole globe. The NP says *eyeball*. She is beautiful and shockingly thin. The effect on her facial features is refined and dramatic, but the bones in her wrists and hands are startling. She reports that as a child, she starved herself nearly to death when her mother declined to support her vegetarianism. It was a battle of wills, she tells me, her mother's will primarily being not having to act as a short-order cook. No one, of course, wants a child with principles. I am about to ask how did it end, this culinary standoff, when the nurse comes in. Johnson, she says. Ten eighteen. Meaning time of death. We write the death certificates and call the families. I am so sorry, I say, again and again.

We are, though. I mean, I am. I often want to ask the other trainees how much they can still feel after twenty or thirty repetitions. What awakens in me is not the memory of my own recent loss—but it is the same feeling, after all, the same tearing pain in the chest. Suddenly the NP bursts out laughing. No, she says when I ask her why, it is terrible. I used to have nightmares that my patients would die, she says. But now I have nightmares that they will not! We are both suffering through one case in particular, a woman revived after nearly bleeding out from a cavitary lesion in her lungs—literally drowning in her own blood. Tuberculosis in this caustic severity is uncommon enough in America that she had, for a moment, been a spectacle. Students lined up to put a face to the scans. In real life, from what we could tell, she had not had, for her one decade of adulthood, at least, stable housing. She has cachexia at baseline from AIDS, now worsened from months and months in the hospital. All of her muscles are wasted away, even the muscles of her face, her temples. Her arms and legs, in contrast, are bloated, distended—fluids filling what we call the third space—and wounds in her heels that go down to the bone drain serous fluids onto pads on the bed that the nurses change six times a day.

This woman seems to the NP to be a worst-case example of dying badly. I am not so sure. Because of the physiology of what occurred. She had essentially bled out, as we say, and although she was massively transfused, in the interval when her blood by volume was not sufficient to carry oxygen to her brain, she had large ischemic strokes in every vascular territory. So in a manner of thinking—not mine, but in a manner I am aware of—what we are caring for is unclearly a person, in that it is unclear that she is still present if she is not having any experiences that we can discern from outside. This may now be only a vacant body. Might a bad death require someone to be present inside or at least some external signs of an internal experience? I know what you mean, the NP says. But I did not mean it. When I cannot say for sure if a person is present, I err on the side of yes.

And it is easy enough for me and for the NP, both of us the kind of people who apologize to chairs we bump into, who refuse, despite imminent ecological collapse, to kill the spotted lanternflies they say will eat the leaves off all the trees.

In a similar case, another young person, a man living rough, had been found on the street in cardiac arrest. They get him back but with severe anoxic damage to his brain. They do not know who he is and they can't ask, so they put as his name in the chart the name they found on a food-pantry card, the only thing he had on him. And over his months in bed in the hospital, his arms and legs become contracted—the tendons tense and shorten until, in the bed, he is a small ball of a man, his knees drawn up permanently to his chest, his arms hooked around them. Unlike our woman, who always appears to be resting with eyes half open, this man jolts whenever you make a noise, and his eyes roam blankly, roam without fixation—but you can tell from the scans of his brain that he is cortically blind. His mouth opens and closes and opens again gapingly in a way that looks terribly like screaming. He has a hole in his neck, a tracheostomy, below his vocal cords;

no sounds come out. It takes months to get him a court-appointed guardian. You never meet them, the guardians, though sometimes you have to get one on the phone. They can be difficult to get hold of and en masse have a bias toward long-term acute care, toward sustaining whatever life is left for as long as medically possible.

Amid all of the uncertainty around his condition, I take an odd sort of comfort in knowing that he is blind, and I tell anyone who speculates about his cognitive efforts—he does not regard the examiner, he does not look up when you enter the room: But he is blind! He is blind! The occipital lobes have the densest infarcts. It is the only thing about him I really know. The guardian is a thoughtful-seeming young attorney. When he comes to meet the patient, he is horrified by the sight of the contracted body and the constant screaming movements of the mouth. He is able to ask one question quite directly: Under what conditions would this man be allowed to die?

In disorders of consciousness, a classifying distinction is whether or not you have sleep-wake cycles. Anyone who has rapid eye movement in sleep is dreaming, and you can see rapid eye movement on an EEG. You are considered more meaningfully alive if you can dream. Why anyone dreams, however, remains a realm of largely unserious speculation. It is generally accepted that our dreams somehow consolidate our experiences or are used to practice emotional encounters in a neutral cognitive space. The amygdala sleeps when you are asleep, so you can dream about committing a murder, say, and hiding a body, and while you can feel guilt, alarm, despair, it should not be on the scale of what you would feel had you killed someone in waking life. Another theory is that dreams keep us from going blind. We spend a third of our lives with our eyes closed, and the brain is plastic; it learns, it changes shape every day to do more and more of whatever it does already. For instance, in experimental settings, a subject who has been blindfolded for days on end can learn to read Braille faster than a sighted control. Functional MRI demonstrates that the blindfolded subject's visual cortex is rapidly recruited to the spatial role and reroutes to the fingertips to sense small bumps on the page. The speed of this recruitment suggests an argument for dreaming: that the brain plays movies, clips, displays its stray contents, to hold on to neural real estate until we come back into the light.

Not very interesting, says Brother Emptiness when I share this dream theory at the monastery. I think he means it is all too pat, too much mechanics. But I like to think of the brain playing film reels for itself at night, the content elliptical or meaningless, with no other goal than to keep the theater open.

The woman with tuberculosis does not have a guardian. She has a name, a family—although the family has not seen her or heard her voice in many years. She is a grown woman, but when I talk to them on the phone, you can tell from their voices that the person they imagine they are speaking about is a child. I find I can stand at the foot of the patient's bed and, using those voices, imagine the child that she once was. I try to hold that in mind all at once with the half-open eyes and weeping ulcers. I share this practice with the NP. I don't know, she says, crossing her polite tendency to agree with me. I'm not sure you should be doing that.

In addition to practicing Chinese medicine, my acupuncturist is a student of the Western zodiac, Aztec mycology, and kabbalah. He is a young blond, blandly handsome. The new year is the Year of the Water Tiger. It is, he says, in your case auspicious. I am always facedown when he speaks to me. While he speaks, he lines my back with needles, sets up hot glass cups. He is from Utah, raised in the Mormon Church, likable, if you like people who want you to know everything about them all at once. I do. Five of his parents' seven children turned out queer, gay, bisexual, or transgender. But the parents are very supportive. He tells me I was born at the start of Sukkoth. I picture the lemons piled high in the Williamsburg market, the finest lemons for the finest families, some running hundreds of dollars apiece. Ethrogim, he corrects me, *Citrus medica*. He puts the headphones over my head, droning electronica, and asks me to welcome the surrounding light. Do the needles treat grief, I ask him once. He tells me grief is stored in the lungs. But it is not a sickness, he says, lining up pins in my shoulders, down my back. It is not a sickness, just a place to not get stuck.

What was she like, I ask, when she was well? This is to the woman's family, the patient with tuberculosis. It is another line from communication training. Sometimes the families look pained as they answer the question, but I use it to move their minds away from the body and out of these awful rooms. It does not work with this family, though. We are on a video call—the injury, the hemorrhage, so long ago now, and the family live in another state; they can't just wait forever for the end to be over. They slip in and out of the present tense: She's been, oh, you know. She's a very troubled person. Kept to herself, private. She worried a lot that she was a disappointment to us, her father says. Well, we disagreed with a lot of the choices she made. Time to take some responsibility— what could that even mean in this context? They are the ones with a choice to make. What the daughter has now is chronic critical illness. She would be im-mobile on a ventilator for the rest of her short life. Or they could stop it, the family could, tell us to make it stop. How odd, how mean of us to pose it as a choice: In what way would you like to have her die? Usually the families who struggle most with this are devoutly religious. It is hard for them to know if the doctors are God's actors or his obstacles.

There is a tense and harried social worker on the unit whose only job is to guess who might survive long enough to overstay their welcome in the hospital. Her role is to plan nonterminal dispositions. She has an eye on the woman with tuberculosis. That family, she keeps saying, they aren't ready, they aren't ready to decide anything. They are too frail, she says, although I do not know how she knows anything about them. She means they are taking too long to decide about what we do not call pulling the plug. The patient has been on our unit for about four days—the average stay is three—and it is time, in the social worker's mind, to consider referral to a long-term vent ward. I have never been to one but imagine them with horror, for some reason in gray scale and slow motion, an assembly line set in reverse, short-staffed, slow nurses going bed to bed, turning the bodies, wiping the wounds. What is the rush, the family says. I do not know what to tell them. But this is true: she could die at any moment. Not alone, her mother says. Of course she can and does die alone, quite suddenly that very evening, while her parents arrange travel from states and states away. In the end the nurse just hands me a sticky note on which is written the time of death. Would you call them, I ask the social worker, although it is my job. No, she says, and leaves.

The NP is telling me about a part of her childhood when she was in a sex cult. Not the worst kind, she says, not the kind where they actively incorporated the children. The hardest part, she says, was you never knew where your parents were. We have been talking about therapy, something she has avoided since the court-mandated sort she underwent when the group dissolved and her father was sent to prison. Take a fact, she says, that you could never integrate into your life and have a stranger say it to you over and over. Feel the way it makes you feel. What kind of task is that to ask of a child? All he had been charged with in the end was embezzlement.

The psychologist I am seeing I see only on video calls, which I often make into telephone calls so as not to have to always see, in the corner, my own little face. I get the sense she likes it if I can make my voice break, cry, which I can some weeks but not so much others. She sometimes asks me pointed questions about what I do at work and listens while I recount at length a particular person's dying. When the families prefer not to be present, this somehow offends me. Or *offends* is a word too strong. What it does is break my heart. I do, though, understand the principle. It is not uncommon for someone to say: I don't want to remember him this way—meaning the father or brother or son and the way he is being bloated with IV fluids with his eyes popped open and his corneas scratched and covered in petroleum jelly or whichever set of horrifying specifics. When patients are dying of the virus, they are often alone, even now, because of the practical implications of contagion and the shame of succumbing, at this point, to a disease meant to kill only the very old or otherwise inadequate. The first few deaths I saw in this pandemic setting horrified me, perhaps because I was too proximate, unsafe, exposed—and isn't this what scares us most about death, about being near to death, the stark fact of being ourselves unexempt? How good, then, through this exposure to have the learned ease, inoculation, now to be accustomed to the N95, now to sweat less under the gown. In all this protection there is no need for courage as we perform the procedure of extubation. Liberation from the vent, some people call it, but this phrase is vague, too value-ridden, too much poetry. I always pity the body in these cases, a pity so desperate it edges on disgust, self-disgust, a tortured form of empathy. Here is the body alone with whatever of the mind is left—not person enough to bother with attending to? Or just not worth the attendant horror? I stay when I can, prevent this penultimate abandonment. But sometimes I wonder: Who do I think I am? To hold a hand in that instant, to place my own hand on someone's head, to smooth the hair. What an assumption—that anyone would even want that.

Some prayers, of course, are futile: May my body not get old. May my body not get sick. Things happen not because of will but because of causes for the most part outside our control. An odd state in which to privilege autonomy.

Full Code

Sarah is behind in school in every subject. During the lockdown, we had no curriculum. She was four. Now her teacher keeps her after class each day, set aside, and keeps me after I come to pick her up. With a tone of shock, the teacher asks questions: Can she rhyme? Does she know her left from her right? I didn't know that this was what mattered. I taught her chess, like I said, and at night we work on aphorisms. What would I mean if I said people in glass houses shouldn't throw stones? That the grass is always greener on the other side? Some are harder than you might think to boil down to their essence. But she believes me when I tell her no one is perfect, and everyone wants the things they do not have. I always confused my left and right, too, until I was in medical school learning radiology, where the represented body is always to be imagined as if supine in a bed that we are standing at the foot of. We are taught to reference left and right in the orientation of the patient's body, a habit that has left me even more bewildered in the regular world, reaching my right hand across my own body at a diagonal to point to the painting's right, the television's right, which is the left, Eli tells me. The relative direction is cross-applied, he explains, only in the case of a person. To have your own set of relative directions requires that you have a mind.

When I play chess with Sarah, I can see her thoughts, watch her distill the world of the board into a single, fallible hope. To promote a pawn, in every case. I have read it would be harmful for me to let her win, so I don't.

In me, around me, from an early age, my father shows no signs of interest. I receive only the run-off of what he does with my brother. He teaches my brother chess, so my brother teaches me, later and alone, only so he will have someone to practice on. I am barely even suited to this, my moves too erratic and impulsive to hone strategies against, my ambitions in every case obvious and easy to obstruct.

That my father would neglect me seems like the natural course at first, almost consensual, and then I notice that he attends to the daughters of his friends, teases them, comments on their dress. His friends have beautiful daughters. Once I am sent outside to play with one. She ignores me, stands with her back to me, pretends to study a leaf. When I ask her to swing with me, she calls me trash, so I check that no cars are coming and then shove her into the road. I try to become something that might chalk up to good for a girl in our town. It won't be looks; it won't be athletics. I am tone-deaf, hopeless on the clarinet. I cannot act or debate; I wilt under any attention. So I try to get a piece in the art show. I make a statue of a woman with wire, wet paper, and glue. I have, though, no sense of proportion. The breasts are too large, the shoulders too broad, the arms so long the statue falls forward when I stand it up. I cut the arms off. What's that, my father says when I show him. Some lesbian shit? From the last time I go home until the time Eli meets my father, it is years, many years, the life span of a short-lived dog. I have not become a beautiful woman, but I have come to have a beautiful woman's husband. My father seems impressed by this and then provoked or threatened. He takes out a picture of me he took the last time I was home, taken from across the table at a Mexican restaurant. I remember him asking the waitstaff to explain each dish, pronouncing the *l*s in *quesadilla*. When we rose to leave, he put my coat on me as if we were on a date. He pushes the photo to Eli, laughing. He says, She has always been ugly but now at least she has a little meat on her. Eli shifts in his chair. I drink the alcoholic seltzer my father keeps for women guests. He only and always drinks cheap domestic beer, a full case he calls a flight pack every night he doesn't work.

A full code means that when your heart stops beating and you are dead, you want the doctors to do everything they can to bring you back to life. This is chest compressions and this is electric shocks. Cardiac arrest rarely occurs in bodies that are otherwise healthy. More often it is in the very old or very ill, people with sepsis and multi-organ failure, people who will die no matter our efforts. Still, we have to ask. I have seen codes run so many times already, and I have done them myself, been part of the team that does them, and sometimes it works for a little while, and sometimes it does not work at all, and in any case in the end we all file out, away from the body, and leave the floor covered in trash, the paper and plastic and little syringes and line kits and tubing for the IVs and the ventilator. That is the full code, I guess, the compressions and the shocks and the ventilator. I have never seen a partial code. Or maybe that is when the families are present, or you get them on the phone and they say Don't, they say Stop, stop now, right in the middle of it. When they say, He's had enough.

For a while after my father is dead, I wonder if this is what I wanted for him. Perhaps I would like to have been there, to have done it myself and shown him what I can do. The huge ribs, the chest. He was larger than any man I have ever coded. The weight you must place on the sternum is tremendous even in the sick and the frail. Success is measured by the depth of compression. Two and a half inches, ideally, the length of a lemon, the diameter of a twelve-ounce can. The teams call us often to talk patients out of being coded when the labor would be futile. The teams hope we can make the patient or the family see the light. But why should anyone have to say it—Go ahead, let me die—go against everything in the animal body and ask for it: Do not resuscitate.

The night he meets Eli, my father tells the story that he always tells about the day we met. It is about six months after his car accident, and I am an infant. Your mother handed you over to me, he says, and you just screamed and screamed. He even screws up his face as he tells it, wails like a baby. I knew right then, he says, leaning into the punch line. I never liked you from the beginning.

When I am small, at his house for the weekend with my brother, he comes into the room where we sleep and prays over us. I know that to seem asleep I have to make my breathing slow and shallow. But it is hard to breathe at all. If he knows we can hear him, he will shift his air and bearing and begin to tell us stories, stories that I believe to be true but will later find out are the plots of pulp novels or horror films: a girl with the devil inside her, a killer who skins women and wears their skin. This one is a closet-light story, he will say when he begins. And he is not cruel. He will even let me sleep with the big light on. When he prays, he asks God to protect us and kisses a saint he wears around his neck on a chain.

It is not the story that makes me cry. It is an old story. I sometimes will feel happy to hear my father talk about me at all. But having Eli hear it—only hear it. In the version I remember, what Eli says is nothing. Oh, grow up, my father calls at my back as I run to the bathroom. Am I crying? He says to grow some thicker skin. It is later, when I am in medicine, a move my father hates, derides, and he calls me late at night to prognosticate my failure and question my concept of money while giving me none to fund the effort, that Eli takes the phone one night and tells my father to go straight to hell if this is all he is good for. And this is the last time we speak to him alive.

Eli teaches Sarah to ride a bicycle. She will not let him take off the training wheels. She will not trust us to hold the bike up while she learns to balance without them. She leans hard at all times to the left. It won't work like this, he says. She is learning only to do this badly. So he takes her little bike and he

89

pulls it apart, takes off the crankset and the chain and the pedals. He takes off the training wheels and puts them in the trash. I am sure this little balance bike will bore her, but she is off on it in an instant, gliding down hills, putting her feet up on the cross-bar, making the serious joyless face she makes when she is trying. I like to see it even more than to see her smile. Because it is so solitary, so self-determined. And the next day he puts the pedals on, and off she goes riding. It is a week before her first fall. She scrapes a knee, a great gray tear in her little leggings, real blood blotting through. She limps solemnly into the house with Eli behind her. He keeps saying I am okay, she tells me, but I am not.

He teaches her other things too, the name of the big bridge and of the river by the woods, the names of the birds there, though beyond robin and pigeon, she never remembers, maybe rarely mourning dove. He takes her to the city zoos, where the animals pace madly on the concrete, picking at their fur. A thousand species, he tells me, will vanish in her life-time. But we won't let her know it. He gives her quarters for the pellet machine, talks her up until she is brave enough to feed the goats, though they bite her when she turns away. Anywhere we walk, I like to fall behind and stop and watch them walk off holding hands.

A temporary daughter. When she wakes from sleep, she has to be held; wherever we are, she will come and find us, without preference, crawl onto one or the other with a kind of entitlement I have never felt with anyone. Her legs even in the time we have had her have grown too long to fold up in my lap. The psychologist loves to hear about my time with Sarah. So rich, she says after I confess any kind of soft sentiment. I do like to stand in the doorway of her little room at night and watch her breathe. So rich, she says, for you to attend to that vulnerability. I do not pray and I do not tell stories. But who does not love to watch a child sleep?

Now I know I will not have children, though I can't say why. This is not a change of heart but a secret I seem to have kept from myself. The distinction is immaterial. Anyone I tell—usually these women friends, usually the moment before they tell me they are pregnant—feels at once I have done Eli an unspeakable harm. I have tricked him. He is an only child, the end, as they say, of the line. But he would make such a great father, anyone laments again, women mostly who are partners to men they suspect will not make good fathers. A good one gone to waste.

Another time I find Eli and Sarah bent over a picture on his phone. From over his shoulder I see it is a picture of a child's polished skull with the milk teeth still in, dissected to show the adult teeth behind them, high up in the face bones. The thin outer layer of bone has been removed to show off the spectacle of the teeth. Maybe, I say, we should not show her things like that. Why not, Sarah asks. Because, I say. How do you get a skull out of a child's head? Thereafter, when she is told to brush her teeth, she shouts, But they will fall out either way! The calls from her father are sporadic and then stop, and we stop talking about when he will come back, and then we stop talking about him at all.

In a consignment shop we buy a book about some children who find the body of a dead bird. The children grieve the bird performatively, sing a song about it, playact a funeral. At first Sarah avoids the book—it is boring, she tells me. And then I find her sometimes flipping through the pages alone in her room, looking at the words that she mostly cannot read. On the last page, the little grave they made is in the foreground, and the children are in the background, playing baseball, getting on with forgetting about the bird and the funeral. How did the bird die, Sarah asks. I don't know, I tell her. We are out by the river, far from the book; these are the thoughts just kicking around in her head. She looks off toward the water. Maybe it got shot with an arrow. And I think of arrows flying through her mind.

What are you hoping to elicit when you ask this question? I keep getting this from my supervising attendings, from the chaplains and the social workers that fill out the team. We need all these specialists, they teach us, because pain is not experienced only in the body. Other feedback is that I am erratic when I lead a family meeting, falling too far from the script. But it is like this: if you are trying to hang an object on a wall, and you lack the device that uses electric capacitance to find the dense parts, the studs, you can use a stethoscope and listen closely as you knock. This is what I am doing, feeling it out, looking for a way through or anything to hold on to. What are you hoping for now, I ask again, again at the bedside. The man makes a gun of his call button, presses it into the soft underpart of his chin. You and me both, says his nurse.

Another day running late for work, I take a taxi. And suddenly, because I am always late, I am always in a taxi, in the light traffic of early morning along the river on the East Side. Once a banner made of a bedsheet is tied onto a chain-link fence: WHAT IS A MAN? A MAN IS HIS HEART. The man stands beside a rolling office chair, sweeping the street with a broom. Lined up on the curb in front of him are five coconuts. The river has too many waves. People, for various reasons, in boats. Is my experience in this moment contiguous with the rest of my life? Later, on the train again: a baby in a snowsuit drinks from a bottle, coughs, drinks again. His fingers make a sign of benediction. The woman with him has balanced on one knee a gallon jug of milk. She looks sad to have a baby. She sighs as she sinks into a seat. I have arrived.

Self-Help

I am not above reading a self-help book, though I am cautious toward anyone who will admit this too readily. I certainly would not recommend a specific self-help book to anyone. The shame is not to need help and admit it but to admit that you hold in any way a hope, even a small hope, that anything you could find between two covers or anything written by a contemporary, some social scientist, some vitamin guru, writing from a desk somewhere in this same awful world, could offer any respite, any practice to heal our present wounds.

One morning during rounds at the half-vacant hospital, postcards appear on the conference-room table, white with a gray-mist overlay like candle smoke; in the foreground, a dove in flight. The postcards are to mark another anniversary of the pandemic. We are in the third year or the fourth year—you have to count it forward from the time when time stopped. In various locations we are invited to light candles for the dead, a toll already well into the millions. We are not allowed to gather. The vigils are drop-in only, the candles LED for reasons of fire safety. The cards invite a wide silence in the room where we hold rounds, less reverence than despondence, like a locker room after a dispiriting loss. It is spring and the windows are open. Amid the rush of traffic is also birdsong, a sense of small movement you can almost imagine is pale-green buds appearing on the branches of trees. Finally, the attending says: It was silent for weeks. No traffic, no sounds of people from the street. Only sirens, always sirens. I would count the trucks as I came in on my bike. The reefers, he means, for the overflow bodies. The window in his office has no bars, no screen. Fourteen floors up, with a view of the Empire State Building. It is open to the warm spring air. I am on an SSRI, he tells me.

We are just another kind of specialist, and this is our procedure, the attendings like to say. On painful occasions it does not matter which of them you are assigned to. Well, an exception. As I find my legs, as I prove adequate enough often enough, prove I can go through the procedures as I was trained to, I do begin to feel more assertive. One day I am with that same attending, the one with the window; we are on together for a weekend on the unit where everyone dies. I am getting tired, I warn him. Sometimes when I am tired, I cry. That is fine, he says. Terse, but he seems to mean it. He sits with his legs crossed and his wrists twisted and his fingers interlaced—holding himself together. At the end of the day, after a really large number of deaths, perhaps five, eight, I say: Well, this was sad, even just by volume. And he is like a man who lives beside the tracks and has a guest point out to him the sound of a train. Yes, he says after a pause, and then says nothing else. Which ones get you? I ask him. Which ones make you feel it? Oh, he says, I always feel it. When someone dies, I ask. Yes, he says, then too.

Fine. In this work, I do not think we should be well adjusted. We are a cohort very good at getting through things. Not just the hospice doctors, who are allowed emotions, at least in a perfunctory way, but all the doctors. Our training is traumatic even in ordinary times. The young doctors now, who trained in the early virus days, who wore space suits to intubate dying patients and then walked home past crowded bars and restaurants, who were accused of deceiving the public, of hiding cures and prolonging intensive-care stays to raise money for hospital executives—we are an even darker lot. The most common mechanism I have seen to carry on is a superficial performance of total self-interest. None of this affects me, we might say at work, and find other ways to defend ourselves: compulsive exercise, binge eating, excess alcohol. Travel is another popular means of escape when the borders are open, the acquisition of experience: Never been to Reykjavík? Never been to Bali? You have to go, you must.

Even our section chief somewhat publicly loses his mind in an early surge. In his luxury condo building he steals from an alcove in a common hallway a small bronze statue of Christopher Columbus and destroys it in misplaced solidarity with an uprising caused by the brutal public murder of a Black man by police. He is arrested eventually, though the charges are light. In lieu of an excuse, he says only:

I have seen so many people die. Once or twice a year the cases will spike—this is the last time, they say each time on the TV news—and all our veneers of coping crumble, and the tone of the ward shifts to silence and grief and the cloudy carelessness of pushing through parallel hangovers. We do not, as a rule, console each other. Whatever we have been through, we have been through alone.

What Eli sees at work I can barely stand to imagine. The people I meet are always, at worst, dying, definitively still alive; they are temporized on ventilators, suspended in time, where the facts of the matter can catch up to the family. The worst of his work involves the suddenly, surprisingly dead, victims of shootings, falls, freak accidents. His role is to be with the families in those quiet rooms adjacent to the emergency department, in each wail an instance of scalding, incoherent grief. Sometimes it is even children, children drowned in bathtubs or children struck by cars or children who have bled into their heads from unknown coagulopathies. And here he shows up for it. I have wondered how it changes how he sees her, Sarah. I do not ask but imagine from my own work it may be easy to imagine her sick or dead, as I do one day when she arrives home from school with a vomiting illness, wakes us in the night to vomit all over her bed and down the hall and in the sink in the bathroom. I lay her in the bathtub and set to work to clean. Eli cannot see vomit without vomiting empathetically. And she lies flat on her back in water just deep enough to frame her face and stares at the ceiling, quiet, accepting everything.

We get Sarah early in the pandemic. Our lives are already unrecognizable. Still, I try not to take her on, try to get out of it. I explore just gently could she go live with our mother, in our childhood home, in the place that made my brother and me both the way we are. Would that be safe, my mother asks, meaning from the virus. She is worried about what a child will expose her to. That year of lockdowns had sent my brother's stable substance use into some unspecified crisis. I have to get help, he says. For what, I do not ask. Not long before, he had asked me as a doctor if I thought a person could get addicted to diphenhydramine. Sarah's mother left them shortly after she had the baby, wanting, it seemed, not even the child as a reminder.

What happened to us, to Eli and me, in the lockdown year? The stores all closed. It was briefly illegal to be out in the street, but this did not apply to us. We were essential. Somehow this was not a dream but a series of facts about our lives. I was learning how to drive, or I had gotten the permit but was afraid to try until the roads were empty and I could practice undisturbed, moving easily on and off the highway. The floods and fires, it was easy to see, would be like this too, would be something we learned to live with, would be a threat from which we would distance ourselves: Not me, not mine, we are so well, we work so hard, we will use our hard-earned savings and move out to the country.

This was the sense with which we left the early days of the plague and entered the rest of our lives, standing in line to get into chain stores, broad shortages of toilet paper, dining chairs, disruptions in the global supply chain. Our bodies learned in that first bad year what the unimaginable future would feel like to live through. And so we began to imagine.

The hospital emptied before the first wave came, the way the tide pulls far, far out right before the tsunami. Where did they go, the regular ill, how did they keep their broken bones and heart attacks and strokes at home? Even the staff went home, were made to, if they could do their work without a bodily presence, including the chaplains, who could comfort over the phone. It is hard now to remember how afraid we were then, all of us, waiting to see how bad it was going to get. I was afraid for Eli, with his bad lungs, a leftover from being a preterm baby. We slept apart and we did not touch each other, this was for months, and I drank a lot of gin I bought at the walk-up liquor store, a barrel set up like a counter in the doorway, the clerk in surgical gloves. I stayed up late reading terrible news and waited for what I saw all day at work to stop. There was never anything to say about it, and Eli stopped asking. And soon enough they brought the chaplains back in, and this was our life now, and we both saw all of it. He would hold the grievers beside their dead loved ones, grievers who took off their masks to bury their faces in their hands and cry.

Even now I will come home destroyed sometimes, or intact but useless. Where the work works upon you is under the level of thought. So you become despondent, perhaps, you become less oriented toward your goals, and then when you are, for example, sick from the amount of Indian takeout you have eaten in despair, when you have that acid brash creeping up your throat at night, if you dare to wonder even by accident why any of this has occurred or accidentally, because of television probably, think about the universe, space debris, coral reefs, you will instantly and strictly experience severe burning pain down both of your arms, which at first seems like an expression of impotent rage or existential terror but is actually carpal-tunnel syndrome, is cervical stenosis, is just pain in the body from all the time spent staring at the screen.

In the new apartment, the corners are not square nor the floors level. There is no clear reference point with which to align the art we hang on the walls. Even the furniture seems unmoored, mobile. The dresser in the bedroom always seems uncentered on its wall, pushed left, the dresser's left, at first like a trick of the eye until on the floor on the right of the dresser scratch marks emerge, suggesting with an external reality what I am beginning to suspect: the dresser is moving. Now the uncentered dresser and the scratch marks make a set of faults I cannot correct. I push the dresser to center again. A rut, I think, will look better than a scratch. A greater sense of intention. In the same way, I am watching our bodies get away from us, Eli's body and my own. Once, fresh home from the barber, Eli comes to me noticing the hair on the top of his head is growing thin in an arc from the brow like a waxing moon, and the hairs there are pale and wiry, and all at once in my mind he is no longer a young man with gray hair, he is a middle-aged man, young in middle age, but all the same. The sunspots I notice first on his hands and arms, more on the left, the driving side. But then I see they are on my arms too. This is obvious, of course, our bodies take on wear. Somehow we have approached and passed the place where I thought our lives would arrive to us, and us to life, somehow finally adequate.

Months and months in, Eli has not met anyone with whom I work or any of the friends I have made since moving back to the city. I am old enough that all my old friends are gone, gone because they have made good on their dreams or left, having surrendered them. Sometimes at night when we have been arguing, Eli will allude to all of the things he has given up at my behest or under the influence of my judgment. These can include, on darker nights, the priesthood. But when I try to pin him to what he has said, I realize that he is speaking in or from a great haze, a wind of leaves and trees and farmhouses spinning, a storm he is in and not behind. And I do not know what I have taken from him. I wonder all the time.

By midwinter the plants have leveled off. Still half dead, still crowding the lamp, but things at last have stopped getting worse. Eli does the watering, doses the foul-smelling algae juice that makes up for the low light. I am the one who does the pruning. I trim the trees for shape and cut the longest tendrils of the pothos to keep it from poisoning the dog. It breaks my heart to throw out the parts I cut, the vines and branches evidence, it seems to me, of tremendous work. I propagate them in jars and vials, use an enzyme to spur rooting that dissolves in the water. I trick the cuttings into going on, new plants to suffer in the darkness. Somehow this is easier than accepting our limitations.

There is a cohort of patients with epilepsy who have had split-brain surgery, where the connection between the two halves of the brain is cut. This decreases the incidence of generalized seizures and can do so with very few side effects. Because the dominant hemisphere is devoted to the production and understanding of language, and the nondominant hemisphere serves a visuospatial function, you can show things to these patients' nondominant hemispheres only, the half that cannot speak, by displaying images in only the left visual field. They will know these objects with a part of the brain that has no use of language. So they will not be able to name what they have been shown, but they can respond to it. They can draw it, for instance, with the nondominant hand, or, in a variation in which they are shown a picture of a naked man, the subjects laugh nervously but are unable to say why. In other experiments, the nondominant hemisphere is given commands to perform actions: Get up and leave the room. And the body will do that, get up and leave. Then, though, the experimenter asks, What are you doing, where are you going? And the person will say, Oh, I wanted a glass of water. Or: I just needed to stretch my legs. The dominant hemisphere quickly offers some made-up excuse.

Death with Dignity

In didactics we are talking about dignity. Someone asked what we should say if patients ask us to assist them in dying or to euthanize them, acts that are illegal for the moment in this state. A lot of the class are firm believers in dignity. They believe it is something they have and something they need to keep hold of. I realize I do not know what dignity is. I try to imagine the opposite. In this work we meet a lot of men, men and women, but mostly men, who are addicted to opioids and then get cancer, unrelatedly, and then no one wants to treat their pain. It is uncomfortable, the fellows largely agree. No use asking for the ten scale, they'll say, it will always be ten. It will be eleven! And I have seen it too: a patient with a substance-use disorder self-sedates with as-needed pain medicine in the days leading to death. How can we say what they intend? Hard to know—this is a phrase we use a lot at work. Different from saying: I don't know. It is not me that is the problem. The thing itself is unknowable.

He keeps falling asleep, the nurse will say. Still breathing, still rousing to light touch? Yes. But what does he have to be awake for? Central sensitization is the name for a trick your brain plays if you try too hard with medications to cover up some untreatable pain. It turns up the signals louder and louder to get past the drugs and let you know the pain is still there. Small pains grow larger, the skin hurts at the lightest touch. The pain makes itself impossible to get away from.

One night before I am even in medical school, I get a phone call from my brother. I have not lived long enough on the better end of my life to stop expecting something bad to happen at any time. I have met Eli, and we have been dating, if that is what to call it, for only a few weeks. My brother has called to tell me that he has been losing weight, that he has been sweating through his clothes every night. I have gone to several doctors, he tells me. They say it is leukemia. I am sitting on the floor of my little room in my shared apartment. I have rented the larger room out to a woman who works in advertising. She shows me on the day she moves in a snake, a small black corn snake that she keeps as a pet and did not tell me about in the entrance interview. When she is not home at night, before I can sleep, I have to open the door to her bedroom a crack and see it, the black snake, coiled in wood shavings, still in its enclosure. I am so sorry, I tell my brother. Tell me what I can do, I say. I fail to ask all of the major questions, about staging, treatment plans. I have not yet learned to receive this sort of news as primarily a matter of logistics. Instead I am left to just feel it, the confusion and sadness. His life has been awful, I think to myself, and now he will die.

It is a lie, of course, though he keeps it up for about a year, a year in which he gains weight and gets married and has a child and gets divorced. This is Sarah's mother, and then she is pregnant, and he needs a good reason, I imagine, to always be in the emergency department, to always be sick in bed. My father believes him, somehow, even after he comes clean, even after he starts his first long run in rehab.

It wasn't true, I tell him once, my father. But he just shakes his head. Fuck you, he says. He's in remission.

On the rare occasions I come to town, I meet my father at the boat shop. I had thought, hearing him name it, that this was a sort of nautical bar, but it was in fact a repair shop for watercraft where he drinks standing upright in a corner, fishing beer from a red Coleman cooler, bothering the men at work patching pontoons and tooling with outboard motors. He never knows what to say to me, a mutual feeling, but once when I am in school, he tries me on literature, Henry James or James Joyce, interchanging them, falling off course, trying to remember, in his words, which was the bigger faggot. He brings up gay men all the time, has a fear, I guess, my brother will turn out to be one and of what it would mean to be father to someone like that. If I am queer, this has barely roused his attention. It would be unimportant, harmless. His vague approval I feel at heart is indecent or pornographic. But the James thing is not meant to be a display of homophobia. He wants me to think he is smart.

The question of dignity sticks with me for days.

I walk through the woods with the dog, turning the concept over. I am afraid I was born without dignity, raised without it, though perhaps, from my work, I have earned some now. A dignified manner, after all, is a matter of behavior. Decorum can be learned. No matter how scared I am, I will not say I am afraid. No matter how much pain I feel, I will not cry out. Children cry, of course, and can still have dignity— I have seen this in Sarah, again a kind of resolve— and animals have dignity without decorum, or at least without language, the ones that walk off and die in the woods alone. The preceptor says that when asked to provide euthanasia, we return the question: Tell me why you ask. Another fellow, mid-career, who worked as an attending through all the early surges, had a wise alternative: Which aspect of dying troubles you most? But I have never met any-one who sincerely wanted me to kill them—not yet, anyway. In the hall sometimes, a family member will say to me, as if we are friends or I am family, Isn't there something we could do to, you know, move things along?

I meet a man whose father went that way. He is an oncologist visiting from Ontario, where physician-assisted death is legal. What was it like, I ask, unskilled as ever at small talk. We are at a bar after a lecture on novel agents for nausea and vomiting. I tell him about a billboard I saw in New Jersey: END NEEDLESS SUFFERING. Instead of palliation, it was promoting assisted death. It was in a hospital bed, the oncologist says, in a clinic. Someone gave the father a bottle of wine to celebrate, and he drank so much they had to wait to consent him. The specialist, the provider, had called the family members only days before, gave them a forty-eight-hour warning. The father was depressed, a type 2 diabetic. Not quite what you might call terminal. The oncologist finishes his beer and orders another. His father had spent lockdown in a marina, living in his sailboat alone, peeing into soft-drink bottles and talking to the gulls. He walked so little, his legs got weak. When they saw how far things had slid downhill, the family moved him into assisted living.

No one knows how to be in the bar, how to be close to each other with our faces out. No one looks the way I thought they would. The oncologist, for example, has a mustache, a joke, almost, on a face I have seen for weeks and filled in so much differently.

A lot of us will put a mask on to walk to the restroom, as though the path through the bar has riskier air. We cannot be unguarded, even if our actions make no real sense. It is not fear and it is not habit. It is something else.

Assisted living ate up most of the father's pension, leaving little for the joys in life. We didn't know he even knew about aid in dying, his son says. His father told the screeners he couldn't walk. He lied and said he didn't eat. They put him on the fast track. You couldn't stop him, I ask. I mean, as a doctor. But the father said if they stopped him, he would kill himself some other way. He told them he had picked out the bay he would drown in. Suddenly anything he was asked to do, he would protest on account of his irremediable suffering— his words or the screener's. Get a haircut, go out to lunch. He called the aide who brought his groceries an affront to his autonomy. What could we do? the oncologist asks. Get him assessed as too depressed to kill himself? I tried. When the doctor did call him back, she assured him her work did not cost her much sleep. It's the families that make things messy, she told him.

113

It was my birthday when he did it, the son says, if you can believe it. But I don't think he realized that. It took the doctor a few tries to get a patent IV, and then she pushed the propofol and whatever else, syringes she fished out in order from a plastic toolbox. The father went to sleep, and then he stopped breathing, and that was that. So what now, I ask the oncologist, but he does not know. He says, I don't think we can stop it. So I look her up later, the doctor who provided for his father. This is what she calls it. She used to do family medicine, general practice, delivered babies. She says this is the same sort of thing. A strange new world, the oncologist says, and tips his beer to toast my glass of water. The father's last words were: Get me the hell out of here.

There is reason to worry. I do, at least, for people on the margins, people who can't walk or care for themselves without support, people who do not have what the doctors think is adequate cognition. Lives the doctors might think are not worth living. We are, in general, an able and ableist group. Already up north they offer aid in dying to people asking for housing or stairlifts, people on long waitlists for limited social resources. A string, say the authorities, of isolated incidents. In didactics, an expert, emerita in our department, gives us a talk on the subject. She tolerates the autonomy argument much less than the younger doctors do. She talks about values and the social good in ways we know are not based in evidence. There is no world in which a doctor could offer death as a treatment for any sort of illness, she says, even to individual patients who really, rightly want it. Not justly, not in a place like this, where people are valued only if they are beautiful and capable of work.

What a soapbox, says the psychiatrist. We are taking the subway downtown from the main hospital to the clinic where we see outpatients, the critically ill who still wear their own clothes. The psychiatrist is one of those tech futurists who think all death is needless, who long to be wholly uploaded to the cloud. He always has a hot new take, remarkable in its inverse proportion of confidence and forethought. You know, it occurs to me, he says one day, I mean, of course in theory, I am opposed to incarceration. I hear it first as *incarnation*; I am briefly eager to see where this is going. Maybe, he goes on, for violent crimes, if everyone with a tendency toward violence, at least enough of a tendency to come to the attention of the legal system, if all of them are behind bars? And prisons of course being segregated by sex, for the most part—if conjugal visits were abolished, then over time you might find by forces of selection that the population at large will become less violent? He says: I am just thinking out loud. He has invented eugenics.

Once, riding in a cab in Manhattan with a charge, a child I nanny, and his mother at a time I now forget so easily, a time when life has little content other than trying to find, make, come up with the money needed to only barely live it, I listen in while the mother explains to him some eccentricities of American incarceration. He has just referred to a cartoon character, a comic-strip prisoner in striped pajamas with a ball and chain, as a bad guy. His mother is on the board of a foundation that teaches poetry on Rikers Island. Not everyone in prison, she tells him, is bad. Some of them have not even done bad things. She is talking about either tax evasion or false imprisonment, I really cannot tell. And the child, who is five, pales visibly and turns toward the window. It seems to him, suddenly, I imagine, that anyone at any time can be pulled off the street and placed indefinitely in prison. The child is Jewish and Christian on both sides. They have a tree up in December in the arched front windows of their brownstone. Don't talk to him about fires, his mother says, not saying the word but spelling it out: *f-i-r-e-s*. I have complimented the tree's unique lighting—antique bubblers in orbs of mercury glass. The kid has just seen a house fire on the nightly news and is convinced this tree will burn down his house. I give him a gift that year, although he wants for nothing that money can buy. It is a novelty penny the size of a child's hand, dull metal, with all the details, the Lincoln head, the memorial, perfectly enlarged. He has no questions regarding the purpose of this object. He says with solemnity: This is my greatest thing.

Samsara

There is one white monastic at the place upstate. He talks more than any of the other monks. At dharma sharing, that father is still trying to find his answers before he takes his family home. They come all the way from Philadelphia for these weekends. They receive private counsel from a senior nun. What does she say, I ask, but then the bell rings, and after the silence the father does not tell me. I am suspicious of myself around him, of what I want to know. We sit in a circle and take turns asking questions. People ask about sitting or about breath, but the grieving father just asks again: What is the purpose of life? And the white monastic says, If I may. He tells a story about a hopeless monk who could not become enlightened, and the Buddha offers him, like, a white rag or something—

118

the white monastic litters his speech with gentle collo-quialism, suggesting constantly that he be taken with grains of salt, a nod to humility to excuse perhaps his constant acts of speech—and a king comes by on a horse, and one or the other of them wipes his face on the rag, which becomes, of course, white no longer, and this, while not provoking enlightenment at this exact moment, is helpful in a general sense overall.

I wonder if the white monastic knows the man has a dead son. After he tells me how it happened, he tells me he is afraid all of the time, most of all when he sees a rope: I see the rope and I am afraid. I wonder where he is seeing rope so often or if he kept the rope in question, keeps it someplace where he sees it often. Memento mori. I imagine his confusion and horror on entering the scene. I will complete his mission, the father says. I will find the purpose of life. The white monastic's story had the gestures of wisdom, anyway. Maybe I am also a little sour that Brother Emptiness was, for so long, a banker. At the last monastery I visited, the Episcopal one farther up the river, I had also been disappointed by the brothers' apparently shameless unseriousness, the catty way they spoke about the neighbors up the road with their garish and lingering Christmas lights. Here at least they have uniforms, soft brown pants and tunic tops, tan knit hats warming their shaved heads on the contemplative walks they take in the woods each day before lunch.

Were you kidding, I ask Sister Empathy. About the bears?

Eli has many friends. It must be the case that while he is away from home, he spends hours with them on the phone or in other places in the margins of our lives; he finds time to maintain friendships while I do not. One of these friends, while I am in fellowship, dies from a cancer that grew in his brain, glioblastoma multiforme. He had only a headache, some trouble with his eyes. For most of the last year of his life he wore an experimental helmet that sent radiation in small amounts into his brain and the tumor at all times. The helmet came wired to a battery backpack that weighed as much as a child. It is easier, he said, to just keep it plugged in. Although he was young, at the funeral I see the other men his age, Eli's age, face the fact of a funeral with slack resignation. It is true we are all old enough to die. Some of the men have coffee in the hotel lobby after the service before they go home, scatter again until the next crisis. They update each other on the details of their lives, their work, their children, of which they each have many. Eli does mention Sarah. He shares an anecdote from when she was new to us, when we were driving her home from the airport to which she had flown as an unaccompanied minor, arriving with small plastic pilot's wings pinned to her coat. We were driving on the highway with her in a car seat in the back. We were new to all of this, we did not know about the switch in the door that turns on the safety lock. Sarah kept shouting: A ghost, a ghost, behind you! But the only thing behind us was her. When we stopped looking back despite her shouts, she opened the car door, in four lanes of interstate traffic, to let out the ghost.

Somehow they come to talk about the places they live as places we all might flee to in the event of an unspecified catastrophe. One of the men has a family farm not far from the city with sheds full of guns and a fleet of ATVs. What does it grow, though? It is a sod farm, he explains. It grows grass.

What I think for just an instant is a bear cub is in fact a poodle belonging to a neighbor, not a teacup one but a small version of a midsize poodle, badly in need of a haircut. There are two, in fact, and they are identical except for their collars, which you can see only by digging deeply into the hair around their necks. When you find the eyes, you can imagine the dogs they would be with their hair properly cut. I find I feel that those hidden dogs must be the true dogs and are sad to be hidden the way they are. The dogs make me think of tomb dogs I have seen in museums with Sarah, the dogs who sleep at the feet of saints and the dogs from shaft tombs of northwestern Mexico, small fat dogs cast in clay or bronze, some in masks with human faces. The dogs were guides for the soul in the afterlife, the plaques explained, or maybe they were food for the journey. In an Incan version of the biblical flood, the survivors sent dogs, not doves, to look for land when the rain stopped. When the dogs returned matted with mud, the flood was finally over.

On Sundays at the monastery, dinner is lazy, mixed-gender, and loud. Because the chatter is mostly in Vietnamese, it is easy for me to remain disconnected from the scene, but I do feel a little conspicuous. After dinner, in the common room, I sit down beside some other laypeople who are seated around the white monastic. Someone asks a newcomer, a woman from Mongolia who speaks seven languages, which had been the hardest to learn. Russian, she says. Because she learned it at age five in the embassy school, by immersion, for the school was considered the best in the district but with the caveat that the classes were taught only in Russian, a language spoken by few native Mongolians at age five. Her parents had not joined her in the task of learning the language. They asked only why her grades were so bad. She liked the clothes, though, the uniforms, gray with red ties. They called the children junior pioneers.

Then the white monastic gets the floor. Before this conversation I did not quite notice that aside from the grieving father, I have been spending these weekends largely without the presence of men. The men who visit the monastery are somehow exactly what you would expect: bad hair, bad clothes, hiking boots at all times. There are better words, I'm sure, for the exact look of American men searching in the East. Like the man in the dharma circle who wants to permanently seize his insights. He is standing by the water boiler and asking the white monastic if grasping of the present is, in fact, the only good kind of grasping. I want to learn more about the monks—they keep saying they have stress, they have worry, just like us, but they never tell us what it is. When one of the sisters sits with me at dinner, I feel childish with nerves. What to ask? What am I allowed to ask? She is called Sister Friendliness and appears pain-fully shy. She initiates what the sisters call a small talk with an air of anxious obligation. She came here three years ago from another monastery, in France. What was it like there, I ask. She hums thoughtfully. A lot like this, she says at last. Bigger.

The white monastic wants to tell us about the Bud-dhist zodiac. It has only three signs: hate type, greed type, delusion type. Which one are you, someone asks. Delusion, he says with confidence. Though named after poisons, each comes with an antidote—or is it a gift? Discernment is the gift of hate, discipline the cure for greed. And delusion? He does not remember. The place is so earnest. Do I want to burn it down? Whenever I meet Eli's seminarian friends, mostly all priests now, I am struck by their obscenity, their common catty interests. It hardly seems to matter to them if God exists at all. They spend more time on the seasons, the rota, the vestments—meaning clothes.

Some Other Gender

I have a dream that Eli is a priest. He is assisting at the altar. Somehow he has come to know that the sacrament is poisoned. So he eats it, the whole host, then falls and strikes his head on the lectern and dies. The dream resumes several days later when I awaken still dreaming and am scolded for unnecessary grief. I wear a ball gown to the funeral. I hear a woman near me say: Who knew he had a wife?

Now there is always a fight at home, when Eli is home, when we are there together. The conflicts center on domestic concerns, housework and whether he should be obliged to do more of it even if I am not. The apartment is always untidy. There are dishes in the sink, streaks of grease at child height along all the walls, dark smudges circling the

125

doorknobs. A woman is more likely to notice these things, studies show. Attention trains itself. Before Sarah, there were no crumbs in the sofa seams, only beard clippings in the sink, yellow residue on the underside of the toilet seat. The kitchen cabinets are filled with ungenerous leftovers: three broken crackers in an unsealed sleeve, a rolled bag of shattered tortilla chips. There is, at last, the matter of the laundry, which Eli will wash but not sort or fold and then pull shirts and pants straight from the pile to wear wrinkled into work, as if he knows (doesn't he?) that his value is not wedded to his self-presentation. Sarah's clothes make a small pile that takes years to go through, matching each set of little socks, folding the tiny underwear.

Worse, though, are the fights about nothing at all, about what to eat or do, about how best to while away our time. Some nights Sarah goes to bed and the apartment is still and we find we are alone in it with nothing to say. It could be me, I mean, it could be that I make things bad, make them worse. And if I tell that story, and then believe it, what am I obliged to do? Sometimes I imagine my life without him, which would be my life, I suppose, with Sarah.

A single parent. I wonder if and when I would become exactly my mother. She left him, my father, before I was born, and the divorce happened only months after. She worked a lot and would come home tired and watch television late into the night, true crime and criminal drama and documentaries about disasters, and I would watch with her, sitting near her, not touching, even if the shows left me awake long after she went to bed. If I tried to leave the lights on, she would come and turn them off, angry to mask how afraid she was of an electric bill she could not pay. Ever since I made it on my own, I have tried sometimes to redistribute the luxuries of my life toward her. She is always cold, has in fact a circulatory disorder that makes her hands turn white and ache, so I gave her a pair of cashmere gloves one year for Christmas. And she thanked me and then hung them by their tags on the tree like an ornament. When I asked about them months later, she said they were lost. She said they must have gone out with the tree.

All our lives she has been like this. Spartan, almost, no real will except for one thing: to have the body she had before she had children. When we

127

were young she was young-woman thin, trying to lose the weight of pregnancy, and then just middle-aged with a middle-aged woman's body. Her interest in weight loss announced itself constantly in a joy-less relationship to food, an avoidance of seasoning. Cabbage soup frozen in blocks filled the freezer. She would eat Olean until her stomach cramped so loudly you could hear it. She keeps, to this day, a small set of bicycle pedals on a stand on the floor by the sofa which she pedals with her feet while she sits in front of the television. This is why she cannot quit smoking, she says, her weight, how much harder it would get to slim down. She asked if I thought she was at risk for stroke, if she should take a daily aspirin. Nicotine patches give her nightmares.

All she wants—I cannot know this, but I must be close; it must be, at least, a good guess—is that at-tentive, all-allowing love that some animals get from their parents, a love she could not give anyone and that I also crave and cannot find inside myself. When I first learn about epigenetics, about cell memory, this is what I think about, our mother methylating her histones and ours to keep us tense and cold if it is safer, locked up in ourselves. She has placed terms around the situation of her life that form a comfort-ing confinement. The thing she says most often is: This is who I am.

On nights like this I sometimes feel it clearly, that I have to get rid of Eli to save him, that I have to make him leave. But these nights so often follow days with a spousal death at work or always follow just after a deathbed marriage that I cannot tell if I am finally altruistic or deeply unfulfilled or if I just want to get rid of everything that can be taken away from me, to tear it down until I have nothing, want nothing, have nothing to lose.

The story I make up about the marriage becomes the defining story of my life. We no longer have sex, for example, at least for the most part, which I understand is a common problem in a long-standing marriage. I can't, he often says, and this proves true and is a side effect of the medication that he takes for his mood. But sometimes he will say, I do not feel close to you, which I also feel, a condition I mean with my advances to rectify. It does not seem to work that way. Mostly I take care of myself. What I do with my body is imagine it is not my body. Sometimes this means imagining it belongs to someone else, and sometimes it means imagining it is a different body, a man's body. I always feel a crude despair when I am done, that moment right after, when sad knowledge settles over me. What I know is that I need more, and maybe I mean more joy or pleasure, but sometimes also it feels like I need another body, meaning unclearly my own or another's, I need to feel it, reach down and touch it, and have it really be there. It may be dysphoria, the psychologist says, but it is not clear that it has an impact on your day-to-day life.

While Eli is in seminary, he spends more time in prayer, in meditation, some kind of Western meditation that I do not understand. He tells me one day that something occurred in one of these sessions, has happened to him, and what he describes is essentially a religious vision. He can tell me almost nothing about it, staggers through the vaguest description. It disperses under language as all things outside this world do. Even the sense you might have in a moment, waiting, say, for the light to change, and with closed eyes you might see the sun glowing through your eyelids—even this could not exist in language if whomever you tried to speak it to had never closed their eyes and looked through them at the daylight. A sort of presence, he says, benevolent. Like a man? No, well, no. It was a sense of God, I know he thinks this at the time, though shortly thereafter he seems to forget that for a moment he was almost sure.

I have never had a religious experience, though I once saw the ocean, the Pacific Ocean, and wanted in the purest way to die. Now Eli tells me he thinks about dying often, almost intrusively, as an alternative to thinking other thoughts about the contents and logistics of his everyday life. It is better now, he says, since he started medication. You can tell it is better, he says, because I am telling you about it. This is true, at least from what I learned in medical school. I know a validated scale to assess his risk of attempting suicide and his statistical likelihood of succeeding. His biological sex, his age, work against him. Of course he does not own a gun. I wonder if I would be able to turn him in, though, hand him over to the doctors, even if on paper things have begun to look pretty bad. I try to imagine what it would be like to lose him like that after living so long amid all his red flags. Do you have a plan? I ask him. Of course I do, he says, and then he laughs.

A bird should not fear the destruction of its cage. Someone says this, a priest, I guess, at the funeral of a child with a genetic condition that bound him to an electric wheelchair. The funeral is broadcasting to Eli's phone. I do not go to many funerals, or where else would I go? But Eli goes to all of them.

A woman dies, my same age, and while she is dying, her husband brings their child in to see her. The child is a baby and the woman is in a coma. Well, *coma* is not really a medical term. She is obtunded, does not rouse to voice or light touch. I cannot say it is right or wrong to bring the baby. He walks, actually, walks badly. He is a toddler. The woman dies the next day, with only the adults in her family in the room. What should we be looking for? her sister asks before the end. Her sister's hair, like the baby's, is red-brown and curly. The dying woman, the now-dead woman, has no hair on her head at all, not even brows, not even lashes. I will lose my hair, says another woman, again about my age. She is holding some of it in her hand, looking at the ends. It is long and brown, blown out. None of this matters, she says. That's what my mother says to console me. Only survive, nothing else matters.

The permissible pleasures, the pleasures of renunciation, are sometimes called unearthly pleasures. But Earth is the only place most of us will ever be.

I was with a woman for a while the first time I moved to the city. I mean, we were dating. This is the closest I have come to being a man. She was an artist, a painter, sharp-eyed and a little mean, with that mystic self-assurance I did not know at the time comes only from money, from always having had it. And one morning toward the end we were sitting on a beach in the winter, somewhere on the coast of Long Island. It was very cold, and we had both been awake all night, except I had slept a little on the train we took to get out there. I was making up a story about how we would end up together. We were already together, but there was a tenuousness to the arrangement, and she was very unhappy and very unyielding and had begun to go to bed at sunset and make me go with her, saying, What else is a couple for but that no one sleeps alone? In the story, it was the distant future, we were middle-aged, and we would meet on a beach like this one. I would be a famous novelist and she would be a painter; we both would have done well in the young lives we

133

lived separately. We both would have been smoking cigarettes, so I add them to the memory. I cannot imagine she has quit, as I have, for my health, for the health of those around me. The beach is an ashtray. The sand is white, fine as dust. She would be married in our imagined future, but the wife would be done away with. How, she asked. I will have a lot of dogs, I said, and the dogs will eat her. She seemed pleased with the fantasy as I spelled it out. I was seventeen and she was only a little older. She seemed to like the idea that I would never recover from her, from our time together. Her top front teeth sat directly on top of her lowers and were foreshortened by how she ground the top and the bottom teeth together.

I think about her sometimes, only rarely, really, not more than once a month. From what little detail I know of her life now, it is an artist's life, labor, obscurity, roommates. I am the one who squared up and sold out. Married a man, became a doctor, acquired complicated finances with poor liquidity. I do have the dog, just the one, who does keep me from meeting anyone at all in the street, acts as though he will eat anyone who comes near me, even to ask the time of day. So what does she have that I want? And who is the wife to be eaten?

We met up again, not recently, but as adults, when I had first gone back to school. We sat in a park and ate sandwiches. When we were in line at the deli I told her I was doing the prerequisites to study medicine. She laughed out loud. I managed to respond with a tone of curiosity, though of course I was offended. She insisted it was only that she had been sure I was joking. On the bench for some reason we talked about the time she met my father. I remember very little about the encounter except that my father was embarrassing; he had behaved quite caustically, and whatever I had wanted her to learn about him or about me in that encounter had not been delivered in any form. I did not remember, for instance, that my father had told that same story, the one about my infancy, meeting me, and just as when he told it to Eli, it had made me cry. But in the park that day she recalled the incident with uncanny specificity, how I had run into the bathroom, how my father had sneered, said, Grow some thicker skin. He was harsh, she said. But you seemed to want him to hurt your feelings.

It did seem there was something I did to men or around them that provoked a kind of violence—a classmate in undergrad once told me I looked like someone who liked to get hit. But he was diagnosed with a brain tumor not long after that, so maybe, like my father, he was suffering from frontal disinhibition. That does not mean that what he said is wrong, only that he should not have said it.

Eli meets this woman once, the old girlfriend. She has paintings up in a warehouse out in an outer borough. In the crowd I find it pleasant to try to see her; in every instant that I find her, she is in intense conversation with someone dressed for the scene in formless linens or high-end streetwear, with a bad haircut, tattoos up the neck. She holds herself neurotically, arms close in, crossed tight, shoulders hunched forward. When the two meet, Eli addresses her with the gentleness you might use to speak to someone who is very ill. She looks defeated in advance, attempts something like sarcasm. It falls so flat that it is only a source of confusion. The art itself is just shapes in bright colors, surely nothing more than run-of-the-mill, but I can see her in it, a consistency of line or vision amounting to something like voice, and what I feel is a longing, for what I am not sure.

On the subway platform Eli is withdrawn, and when I ask why, I find that he is angry. It was awful, he says. I hated everything about that. That woman, he says. And the way you looked at her.

The most beautiful man at the monastery is from Bombay. At orientation he confesses he is considering renunciation. I have come only from violence, he says. He wants to find a way out. He sits beside me as Brother Emptiness gives a lesson on meditation. All our lessons are on meditation, and all such lessons are the same. Breathing in, I know I am breathing in. Breathing out, and so on. Brother Emptiness recommends counting the breaths, not saying to what number. When the talk is over, he takes questions from the small crowd circled on cushions around him. When I count, I can focus quite well, but I am focused only on counting. At three, I remember two and look forward to four. I always want everything to be over. I ask what to do about that. You count when you are beginning, says Brother Emptiness. Later, you stop. This is the whole of his answer.

But the beautiful man catches me later, after an

hour of group exercise in which we swung and lifted a long light stick like a gondolier's pole. He says: Are you counting with words? In English? I am, I say, yes. He says, Try this, and produces a notebook. He begins to count while drawing figures: empty circle with a vertical slash, filled circle with a vertical slash. The same arrangement with a dot in one or another corner. Isn't it just more symbols, I ask. Like binary, he says. Do you code?

I dream I meet my father on a train. We have already met when the dream seems to start; we are sitting in the sightseeing lounge where the windows bend up into the roof. The newspaper rustles crisply as he folds and unfolds it. Can I ask you something, I say, but he does not look up. Are you afraid to die? Oh, no, I am making this up. I have never dreamed him on a train. But I would ask him, I would want to know. I imagine at that point his vague religiousness would have emerged. Who was this guy who wore a saint around his neck, who had an old priest he would call late at night, who got drunk every night and prayed over his children? Well, he doesn't take my calls much anymore, my father said to Eli, whom he had begun to call Reverend, uncorrected.

In one dream, in his house again, he is still dead but tells me, smiling, Now I know I will never die.

On my way to clinic, midday, I hear a man shout-singing through Union Square: I've seen this happen in other people's lives, and now it's happening in mine. It is cold and the air smells like burning cinnamon. Mormons on missions loom over businessmen with their lunches, trying to spread the word.

The weekends I spend away are short, but longer at night, when I sleep poorly in my little bunk and dream troubling dreams. It is too dark in these woods, surrounded by strangers, lying on thin mattresses on thin wood slats. Everywhere at all times the doors are unlocked. I move myself from the hall bed I was assigned to into an empty room. Sister Mindfulness Observer looks for me in my old spot and signals disapproval when she finds me elsewhere. But no one else is coming until after I am gone, I say, though this is not the point. In the empty room I close the door at night and lock it. I worry that this violates some sort of code. The information sheet says, in the passive voice, DOORS REMAIN UNLOCKED, and though I have proven this not to be true, I have not harmed anyone; in fact, no one should come to know what I have done, for why would anyone, if it is so safe that doors may remain unlocked, try the door in the night in this quiet building, this sort of house, the only time that I have locked it? I lock the windows too, but all the same I cannot turn the lights off to sleep. I try as a practice to sit in the dark and cannot last five minutes, and while the lights are off I cannot close my eyes for fear that in the double darkness in an empty room with a locked door and locked windows, something will sneak up on me.

In addition to seated meditation and walking meditation there is working meditation. I am raking leaves with the woman from Mongolia and another woman, who is tall and stooped and always wearing noise-canceling headphones. I sense you have an unattractive tendency to find others disappointing, the Mongolian woman says. We are gathering leaves on tarps and dragging them to a forest clearing to rot without souring the rolling green of the lawn. Along with the leaves are hard green tree nuts the size of golf balls that she insists we leave to nourish the wildlife. But the nuts collect in unsightly piles as we rake; they are eyesores amid the waves of combed grass. I decide to scatter them back into the field. This is what provokes, obliquely, the woman's comment. But the woman in noise-canceling head-phones squats beside me. Throwing and throwing the tree nuts, she says to no one: I have never been happier!

Mortality Class

Wherever I find you, turn off your video, close your eyes, and focus on your breathing. Resolve yourself to be here now.

I have a patient who is also afraid of the dark. No, this is new, she tells me, when I too quickly admit in a general sense that the dark is essentially frightening. She used to be a city planner. Now she is bound to an electric wheelchair and for more and more hours a day—her latest estimate is nearly twenty—wears a rubber mask strapped tightly to the face with an articulated hose connecting it to a machine that forces air through her mouth and into her lungs. She cannot do it on her own, breathe, or turn on the machine, or turn it off, or reconnect the hose if it gets disconnected. She has amyotrophic lateral sclerosis. When I ask her the values questions, she says: It matters most to me to maintain a positive attitude. Okay, I say now, why are you afraid of the dark, the night? I am afraid to sleep, she says. I am afraid I won't wake up.

We are taught to elicit these hopes and fears with scripts of specific questions. It is less obvious what we are meant to do with the answers. The naming, we are taught, contains an innate value. But no one ever said what it was.

Once in virtual mortality class we are asked to list the things we value most, five things in four categories, so twenty in total. The first three categories are People, Activities, and Parts of the Body—I struggle to complete the assignment. Who, for example, values five parts of their body? I settle on the senses. But the fourth heading is Values—values you value? I write *presence* and then run dry. Then the facilitator solemnly reads a disease course of a woman with cancer, written in the second person. In the shower one morning you notice a lump. After every line or two, the facilitator says in a tone of high seriousness: Cross one item off your list. I cross out all my blank lines and then move on to People. I cross out Eli, then cross out Sarah.

Most of the fellows will not be hired on. These are lean years for the unessential specialties. We are often clustered with spiritual care, music therapy, and the volunteers who come in with docile dogs or crystals or do Reiki. The fellows who will stay, it seems, are the ones who call the department heads by their first names while referring to their research by date of publication. Throughout the years of training there are instances when the track ends or there is a gap in the track, a place where one might fall off course or become irredeemably lost. At this point I always feel I will, surely this time, be found out, discovered as fraudulent and evicted from the field. This does not occur, of course. My sense of displacement, I am told, comes from a poor internal sense of assurance and is not related to my gendered socialization or the treatment I receive at work.

The NP asks me, Can anyone be happy in this job? We are sitting on the steps of a large church near the hospital. It seems as though we should be smoking cigarettes, but she has never smoked, and I quit a long time ago. I thought it would be different, I tell her, that someone would have shown us how to be. Instead we are the same as any other doctors, any other specialists, performing our assessments, saying the lines, doing the small and small that is expected of us. Leave what is not yours, someone is always saying, but I don't know what that means.

Before disclosing difficult information, we are supposed to ask the patients, the families, Would it be all right if I shared this with you? The question feels unnatural at first, or socially odd. And what if they say no? That is easy, it turns out. If they say no, you just stop. If brave, you can venture, Tell me more about that. We are also supposed to ask, always, how a patient likes to be addressed. Almost no one does this. We largely revert to calling a person by their surname and presumed title. But I have come to like calling people by their first names. People with brain injury, for example, who are otherwise unresponsive will sometimes rouse only to the name that their mothers called them. So I am trying to ask. What should I call you, I ask the man who is new today in continuity clinic. The question lands wrong, seems confusing. I try again. What do you like to be called? Well, says the man, who is standing when I arrive even though he has been alone in a room with a diverse array of chairs—an examining chair with a paper cover, a plain office chair set beside it, a rolling stool near a wall-mounted computer. You should know my name, he says. It is in your paperwork. Of course, I say. He goes on as if I were very slow. It should be the case that you call me Mr. Smith out of respect, for a time, and if over time we become close and develop a rapport, you might begin to call me John. Though curiously, throughout all that time, I will still be obliged to call you Doctor.

Mr. Smith has spent most of his adult life in prison. I do not ask for what. This is something I learned not from communication class but from television. All he offers is that he didn't do it, the crime he was convicted of. After parole he was diagnosed with cancer of the stomach. What do you hope for now, I ask. I want a normal life, he says. And what would that look like, I ask, and he only laughs. Can I argue ingenuously that the title is helpful, that it holds a power to help, even a power of placebo? The title and the space it conveys around me, the distance. Yes, I could make myself believe that. I wear the coat too.

He does share one hope. He says: I want to matter, to know that I matter. And I follow up as I have been taught: What would achieve that state for you? How would you go about doing that? He comes back once more and then he never comes again.

An overarching concern is that we are burned out, physicians, because we no longer find any meaning in our work. A study concerning selection of medical specialty outlines the following interests by which a trainee might find a job they will go on to tolerate from the perspective of meaning:

Opportunity for Decision-Making
Opportunity for Expertise in a Specialized Area
Opportunity for Research
Opportunity to Make a Difference
Opportunity for Control

Most of us, if asked directly, would not say that our lives are meaningful only to the extent that we control them, though perhaps, if this is true, we should start saying it.

A man on the subway is pleading for food. He says: I used to matter, I used to be somebody. He is as confused as the rest of us.

I am afraid to die. I'm sure it goes without saying. I

sometimes have a pain in my eyes and also a condition of the pupils which appears in certain light, conditions always present in the windowless restroom I use most often while I am at work. Anisocoria—one of my pupils, the right one, I think, without looking, is sometimes a millimeter or so larger than the other. Does it come and go, asks my favorite neurologist, who is young and handsome and somehow both perpetually joyless and always laughing. What comes and goes, it doesn't matter. He is from Nigeria and he is smarter than all of us. Another doctor I knew in training told me that if you grow up smart in Nigeria, you have to become a doctor; right at the end of childhood they send you off to become a doctor without even asking if you want to go spend your working life tending to the ill and injured. So I often wonder when I meet a Nigerian doctor if they ever wanted to be here in the first place, though I could wonder that about a lot of us. Another Nigerian doctor I met was an unyielding gender essentialist. He would bend himself into strange shapes to open doors for me wherever we went. It is not right, he said once when I bought him a coffee. I pushed on this only a little. He told me that men and women were essentially different, in every case, a biological fact all the way down to the level of our cells. It is not an insult, he offered. In many ways, women are better. Better at what, I asked. He said, Multitasking.

I remain, throughout all of what will be his recorded time, ours, I should maybe say, afraid of my father. He looms over me no matter how tall I grow and seems taller still since he is always standing, something related to a condition in his back, standing in the kitchen, at the counter, standing before the sofa at the television. He would watch sports on television, football, most often, where the commentators on the sidelines were women in contrast to the box commentators and the studio commentators, who were men. The women on the field looked so small next to the players—anyone would. But perhaps the point was that only a woman should be seen that way. My father would speak to the field commentators. If he did not like the contents of what they had to say, he would call them cunts and bitches in direct address. One in particular maybe he would praise, a blonde in bright lipstick. The praise he would offer was: Beautiful teeth.

Studies have shown that women physicians spend

triple the amount of time on household chores than men physicians do. The wives of men physicians are unlikely to hold jobs. Yes, Eli says, I know this. You have shared this with me many times. I have not, I realize, come to terms with being a wife except in that I have asked that Eli not call me his wife, and we were married using the same-sex liturgy, which includes no references to wives, ribs, or women. This is my spouse, he says to introduce me. When we met we both felt ill-suited to our genders. His femininity was a softness, a desire for vulnerability, that the world of men was not apt to accommodate. *Vulnerable*—does this mean easily hurt or easily harmed?

A type of conflict Eli and I used to often have but that no longer arises relates to a large number of traumas I endured before meeting him, which did include almost every type of violence you can imagine. I would have been drinking, we both would have been, and I would be beset by a wave of painful, sullen aloneness, perhaps provoked by a memory that at first seemed safe to examine and then would pull me out like a hidden tide into a sea of enraged despair. When I would remember to notice Eli at all, I would notice that he had sensed the shift and was only afraid, withdrawn in fear, and I would be alone in it, which made it worse. Why did I have to be alone in it? If other people had done this to me, why could other people not undo it? I even endured a brief psychiatric hospitalization in the time that we were first dating. The first thing you have to do is accept that nothing will help.

It never really got wild unless we would drink together, and we do not drink together anymore. What I had wanted to convey, before I stopped bringing it up, was that these experiences were unimaginable and had affected me in unimaginable ways. If I struck him or broke things—once I even took the glasses off his face and snapped them in half, wanting to find an action with memorable, financial consequence—it is important to admit that I know this was abuse. And once we call it that, there is no use in asking what else it was. So often speaking from the other side, I know that abuse is not very interesting. One could take an etymologic interest, maybe. What is it that spousal abuse and substance abuse hold in common besides frequent collocation? *Abuse* as a noun: improper practice. As a verb: to deceive, misuse, use up.

The psychologist says that abused children tell sad

stories about themselves forever. About how they are bad and why and how they have brought bad things on themselves. It is better to be worthless, to believe it, than to suffer for no reason in a world that makes no sense.

I find when I am constantly sober that my impulses are easier to examine. And I can set goals and establish routines, crisp habits; I can reset myself to lesser pleasures and feel largely okay. But also I am alone. I mean, I feel as alone as I am, tied up tight and afraid all the time, and nothing gets better with Eli. Please stop, I say one night. He is doing it again, saying this isn't working, there is no hope for us, everything he used to hope for is gone. The start of this was nothing. A disagreement about a household chore, about television. Please, I say, I am not feeling well. It is true. I am awaiting the results of a viral PCR and furloughed from work until the test comes back. I am on consult service at the community hospital. The intensivists are overwhelmed by another surge. It isn't just the numbers, which are high, or the uncertainty, which wakes our barely rested trauma. So many of the nurses have quit that a third of the beds in the ICU are empty, blocked, cannot be filled due to insufficient staff. The consults have started to seem preemptive, like palliative extubations on patients who have only just arrived, freshly resuscitated. A hopelessness infuses the prognosis. Day two and he will never wake up, the teams tell the families. And we are called to withdraw the breathing tube, to move things along.

This isn't working, Eli says at the end of every fight. Five years of this, ten years of this, add them up and it isn't working. It is sometimes difficult to tell when he is expressing himself authentically as opposed to using weapons I have made for him, given him, instructed him in the use of. Is this just marriage and its discontents?

If you die suddenly, you know no difference between your death and the end of the world. Only this year in this work does this occur to me. Let the world go on as it always has—is this a prayer that will be answered? Still, most of the people I have ever asked say they hope to die all of a sudden, out of nowhere. So there will be nothing to try to understand and nothing to be afraid of.

A Very Private Person

He has no family, no contacts, no representative. The legal term is *unbefriended*. From where I stand in the doorway, I can see he is alert, holds his body in a way suggesting wakefulness. He may be oriented enough to give us a name, to name someone we could call on his behalf. Maybe no one else has tried hard enough—I wonder this, as I often do, and often I am wrong. This man is dying of liver cancer. He is a fit man in his mid-forties, bald but with a good head for it. Handsome, I mean. He appears well kept except for an odd detail: long acrylic fingernails, a few weeks grown out by the gaps at the cuticles. I am so glad you are here, he says at last when he sees me. He reaches for my hand, and I take his, although this ritual of contact is no longer a custom in the hospital. Something isn't right here, he tells me. I have to agree. His skin is yellow and he is yellow in the whites of his eyes. His hands shake in a special way we call asterixis, a slight sort of flapping. Listen to me, he says in a conspiratorial tone. I do. I don't want to die here, he says. Who is your family, I ask him, but he shakes his head, and looks intensely toward the door.

It is no longer clear to him why he is in the hospital. It is hard to get up, he admits, it is getting hard to coordinate the urinal, a bottle with a handle that hangs on the bed rail. In his beleaguered sensorium, the relations between sound and object, inner force and outer action, are disintegrating. The third day is when he sees the demons. They must come from a deep and vivid internal mythology—unclearly religious, superstitious, cinematic. His pupils dilate as his eyes scan the empty room. His syndrome— hepatic encephalopathy—has made him both easily terrified and prone to sudden sleep. As he nods off, like a child he says: They told me to, they told me to. What did they tell you? To tear out my eyes.

His eyes are intact but the acrylic nails have been bitten into sharp points like little shivs. He has been

tied to the bed with soft blue cuffs for his own protection. But they run no tests—he refuses them, the
team tells us. Bulky masses in the liver are causing it
to fail. I want too badly to know about the nails and
to file and paint them or to take them off.

I sometimes see the doctors, the palliative ones
not excepted, find in the family meetings the golden
phrase that means our work is done. A very private
person is the opposite of a fighter, the opposite of
someone who wants everything. Well, you could say
that about anyone who lives on the street if their
tongues were cut out and you had to speak for them.
They wouldn't like this, they shunned institutions,
they were very private people, they didn't even like
being indoors with someone. And that was what his
sister said when we finally found her through some
detective work. Oh, he was a very private person. A
free spirit. A free spirit is what belongs to a body
that is dead. And his was, soon enough. I do not
know why I wondered if she had been wrong about
him, if there were other reasons he had not given
himself to her to be known.

Jaundice worsens, cognition deteriorates. But the
demons recur. He told me to eat myself, he says

one day. Again, again, he told me to tear out my eyes. I think of my father—at the funeral, a priest he had never known at all calls him a restless soul. And in the pew, his primary bereaved, I wonder if *restlessness* is a good word for addiction, an ill ease, a striving, an adaptive form of hope.

One man in his thirties has been in the hospital dozens of times a month for years. He has a psychotic illness, schizoaffective or schizophrenic, and antisocial personality disorder. As a side effect of decades of antipsychotics, he is morbidly obese; like most people with schizophrenia, he smokes cigarettes constantly. He is diabetic; he is, as we say in the charts, undomiciled. His chief complaint on most presentations is suicidal ideation or chest pain. I find his life difficult to imagine, though the internal-medicine resident rotating with us does not. Many of the homeless I meet, she says, seem relatively happy. Some of them have little dogs. We had been discussing a Canadian case where a woman with a condition called multiple chemical sensitivities had chosen euthanasia because she did not have access to a safe, clean place to live. Who would do that, the resident asks. The man with schizophrenia presents again for assessment of chest pain and has a cardiac arrest in the waiting room. He is found pulseless, slumped in a chair. His heart is restarted but he sustains severe irreversible brain damage, and after a few days his family decides that he would not want to live on in this way and that they will remove the machines. This is when we meet him, and them, in the meeting where they say: At last his suffering is over. They are glad it happened this way; at least we can be with him, they say, at least we know where he is and we aren't calling around asking each other: Have you heard from him? Has he called? They survive, find meaning; they will donate his organs. In intensive care, the mood around him shifts; his body, so large, so recently only a problem, is tended to at last with reverence. We have found a use for him.

This Is the Limit
of My Vision

Little flies are coming from the potted dirt the citrus trees grow in. The trees hang on, though it hurts to think of how grand they once were in the good light of the suburbs. First was the lemon tree, Eli's learning tree, which had flowers when we bought it, even birthed some little lemons we sliced to float in glasses of gin. Then the flowers stop coming and the leaves fall off and all the branches shrivel tragically. From the nub of trunk that survives all this is born a different, non-fruiting tree—it seems that indoor citrus trees may be just citrus branches grafted onto hardier ornamentals. No matter. In this house, we keep what grows.

One patient with leukemia is himself a doctor, a general surgeon in practice for forty years. How many appendectomies do you think that is, he asks us, cholecystectomies? Thousands. All he wants to do is get well enough to go back to work. He is divorced, and estranged from his children. I have spent my whole life in OR scrubs, he tells me. My closet is full of fine suits I've never worn, rows and rows of suits in gray and black and navy. I am working with students and ask if he would like to offer them any advice. Yes, he says. What you do for work is more important than who you marry.

Although Eli and I rarely attend functions together at our places of work, when we do, I am always approached by Eli's colleagues with curiosity. There is nothing I can do or be that would make me appear as an apt reciprocal. I sometimes overplay being withdrawn or ill at ease to make the contrast vivid. I share their assessment that he and I are poorly matched. Sometimes I will suddenly realize I cannot see him, Eli, at all. This will happen anywhere; on the subway, say, I will see him all at once as if he is another person, a stranger far from the heart of me. And it shoots so thrillingly through me that I will begin to pretend that I do not know him or that we are old friends, long parted, and he will play along. We will spend whole days like this, go out and come home again, pretending. If I ask him then, Tell me about yourself, he won't, nor talk about his work or his path to it. So we are left to just perform ourselves in the present. It makes me more attentive, and it makes small gestures thrilling, and if it culminates in sex (it doesn't always), the sex is thrilling—something about its being wrong or at least being singular, uncertain to happen again.

When we become ourselves, the next day, or, abruptly, to care for Sarah, or for some kind of household logistic, it goes straight back to how it was, like a habit of mind, like a programmed set of responses, the tense, transactional standstills. Why is it like this? It is no use talking about him, says the psychologist. We can only speculate, and I am obliged to take your side. I have a similar bias. There is an incident with a day we planned to take Sarah to a museum, and somehow in the last moment, it is just Sarah and I, and he clarifies: I never said I would come, only that I might. I did not realize, he says, that it was extraordinarily important to you. So I take Sarah to the museum myself. It is at the top of a tall hill. Options for approach include a gentle set of cutbacks or stairs straight up. Sarah takes the stairs. Her interests at the museum, acutely limited, are nakedness and animals. We count every dog we find. Her favorite thing we see is a statue of a young boy holding an apple, naked, painted brightly. This is, per placard, the child Jesus, but I do not bring that to her attention. I keep trying to pause us, asking her, What do you see? Because she seems for her age unskilled at matching words to objects or experiences. She says: A boy, an apple, he is naked, his ladder is out. Imagine that—it does seem to be something you climb up with.

Afterward, in the park, I see a bird weaving zip ties into its nest. A man in a small crowd of children uses two sticks and a rope to make soap bubbles the size of small cars. He lets the children try it too, shows them how to lower the rope into the detergent, hold the sticks up to let the wind blow through. I wonder if he makes enough in tips that this is lucrative, or if it is merely a way to be close to children. He appears sufficiently innocuous. On Sarah's turn, she tries and tries with the wet rope and gets nowhere. Her technique improves little with each attempt. The man and the waiting children watch with infinite patience. Sarah's hair is bobbed, her shoulders glow white in a little sundress. Her scapulae look like the wings of little birds. At last in a generous wind, she gets it. She regards the bubble seriously as it pulls away from the rope, sinks to the ground, and pops. We pass a statue of a dog on the way out. It must remind her of a gravestone. She whispers, Is the dog dead? I tell her the truth: Yes, it is safe to assume that anyone in a statue is dead.

With Sarah in family places, playgrounds, I will sometimes make stilted conversation with the others, the parents. I don't announce my difference. I take the assumption that I am her mother. One woman I tell for some reason that I am a physician. She says: My wife and I always lament that one of us isn't a doctor. She means to pay the rent. It is clear from her tone that this is something she assumes would have been available to either of them, which more likely means that they are rich than that they are smart. She is a writer, she shares, a novelist. This is another profession anyone thinks they could just fall into. What I lament, though not aloud, is that I do not have a wife.

The psychologist suggested I frame the marital

conflicts as failures of connection. She is an advocate of codependence or at least seems to believe that if present, it must be accepted, its confines worked within. I use the lines she gives me, although I find them too direct. When you don't arrive at the places I expect you, I say, it makes me feel like I am unimportant. He will not answer if I speak to him this way, only sigh deeply and leave me alone.

Sarah is acutely attuned to conflict. She will scold us if she hears us speak in sharp tones. Stop squabbling, she will say, a word we have never said to her which must have come from some other world. And she notices, of course, when Eli doesn't show up at places, when it is his day to pick her up from school and she comes down the stairs, one in a row of little backpacks, and I alone am the stand-in for the family she does not have. She doesn't have to be our whole life, Eli will say, though it seems to me she should be more of it. Or I feel that, on top of my work, I do not have the time for both of them. So on weekends we will sometimes leave her with a sitter for a night, if we have, say, tickets for somewhere adult to be. I wonder what his manner would be with our own children. He comes home from his week away full of painful stories I must steel myself for. His work is not so different from mine, though with none of the clarity or deference or financial advantage that comes with being a physician. I offer support. I name his emotions; I tell him I can only imagine. This takes composure but because of my work, my training, I am able to perform it. The trouble that emerges after weeks of this or months is that this nursing seems to be only the work that was already expected of me. These acts of care in late arrival, that is to say, do not earn me more of anything, any more of any of the things I need—which are what, exactly?

When my father dies, it is the same way. He has enough brothers they are hard to count. They are taller than anyone else at the funeral. The brothers stand tall in the mostly empty room, what is called a chapel, although it looks most of all like a conference room; they stand in their sport coats and are merely present. The performance of connection is put on by their wives, in every case a second wife acquired after my childhood, all women I have never seen before, touching me, wincing theatrically, saying how hard this must be. And it is hard, and

I hate them, these women, the comforters, working outside the world of men.

I try to write a eulogy in the hotel bathtub. We will never know how he died. We arrive on the scene to find it cleaned up already—a brother has taken the cash, the weapons, as if it were the natural thing to do, has cleaned out the kitchen and the medicine cabinet. As I walk through the house, I expect to find my father alive in there, angry to see me going through his things. There is the chair, the carpet dark below it. The hotel bathtub is in the bedroom. This is the jacuzzi suite. The first night I am drunk and Eli is in bed, still sick from the vaccine we both got the day before we left. Tell me what you need, he says. I find I have nothing to say. His suit bag contains a black jacket but no pants, so we go to the formal-wear place to get a rental. I sit amid the prom dresses while he tries on a suit that is nicer than his own suit, the funeral suit he has worn since college. All we do is funerals, says the clerk with pins between her teeth. At the service the men make a circle around Eli, all my father's brothers. They lean in close and clap him on the back. I cannot hear what they are saying. My father's priest won't come to the wake, so Eli says a prayer to close the show in a voice I know from his seminary days.

After this conflict about the museum, I become a ghost in the house. Eli comes to me from time to time wanting to talk about work or with a domestic concern or, rarely, a medical problem. He has a small lump in his left arm, he shares, and nervously he also shares that he has another in one of his testicles. I am divided over whether to make myself useful.

A woman at the monastery shares one morning, regarding the five precepts: When I swear not to kill, I know it means not just other human beings or animals but even myself, I will not kill myself. But it also means I will not let anyone else kill me. I try not to seem to follow her straight out of the room. But when she turns to me back at the bunkhouse, I say nothing. Would you like to hug, she asks me, and I have to trust her in this impulse because it would not have been my own.

Brother Emptiness says to imagine all conflicts from the view of three hundred years. In three hundred years, does this conflict matter? No. He laughs. In three hundred years, we are all skeletons.

Eli and I are at our best just seeing things together:

167

the gesture of a bird, a man on the street with an airplane bicycle made with cut and bent aluminum cans. We laugh at the same things: the face of a man eating in the street, a fountain's stop-start rhythms. And we agree that language is a problem. What else do you need to agree on? There are days when all is well, times we will go off on a little trip. We drive and drive. We leave Sarah with a neighbor. We drive backward into the past. You are so pleasant in a car, he says, because I sing along to the radio, because I fetch him trashy convenience foods whenever we stop for gas. Once, on the very end of the Cape, eating at a small place with a side garden, we both stare with wonder at the sun striking an umbrella on the distant beach such that it seems to glow ultraviolet, and as we stare, the glowing umbrella begins to climb up into the sky. It is the moon, nearly full, rising filled with a reflection of sunset. And in the whole movement from mistake to realization, I feel somehow that I am not alone.

If Eli and I had children, I could tell them the stories of our life, stories that otherwise no one is interested in. It was not a date, our first date, not to his knowledge or mine. I for one felt I was employed in helping someone through an acute physical crisis.

The stressor, oddly, was not internal to Eli but rather related to a friend of his who ran a large nonprofit. The company had made a promotional video related to their cause: helping African children drugged and forced to work as soldiers. And the video, a glossy and engaging production, backgrounded with an up-beat, empowering song by a popular band, attracted so much attention and scrutiny and money to the cause that it caused him, the founder, the CEO, to run naked down the street along a public beach near Los Angeles. No one was harmed. But the event, the occurrence, did raise in Eli's mind serious concerns about his friend's constitution, his moral fiber. It was this doubt and not the event itself that served as nidus to Eli's acute despair. We were both new to the neighborhood, where we lived a long but pleasant walk apart. My door was near a train two stops from his own. I had no chance with a man like him, so through this fact I could not see what it meant when he did not get on the train, when he walked me to my door, when he came up with me to sit on the roof, when we were cold and shared a blanket. We could see the city from there, the heart of it, far off, a few small spikes in an indeterminate glow.

Ghosts

The room has good light. It is a single room in a specialty ICU where people stay for only one or two nights to recover from procedures, stent placements. It is a place people here survive routinely—this means it needs superior decor. The bed is in the middle of the room, and the light pours in from the patient's right side. The patient is dead. He is tucked in nicely under a white sheet and a blanket, right up to the sternal notch, hands covered, eyes closed. I stand at the feet, a clinical habit, pole position for performing a subtle exam. There is nothing to see here. What happened, the son says. He is by the wall, in the corner, the same place he was when I met him, when his father was still alive. You just let him die? For weeks we had been working on this man, for this man, who had become dependent on noninvasive respiratory support, high-flow oxygen that kept him tied to the bed. On the previous day, his last full day of life, the patient told me that for five thousand dollars, a person could go to space. Anyone. To heaven, you mean, asked the wrong-headed nurse. He shook his head, drew an arc in the air with a finger. Up and back down, he said.

Are you happy now? his son shouts at me from the corner in the room where the man is dead. Lurking around here, asking your questions. He didn't want to see you, he didn't want to talk to you. He threw you out. Well, you got what you wanted.

I think this father was talking about parabolic flight, an accessible way to experience floating in space for ten or twenty seconds at a time. The aircraft, shooting through a tall arc, uses the sudden change in vertical load to simulate the absence of gravity. In the windowless padded body of the plane, the passengers are suspended in air, a brief weightlessness that they call, afterward, profound and indescribable. The body unburdened by the pull of the Earth. This may be what that father meant, though the price he quoted was a little low.

An alternative I imagine might have interested him, though at an even higher cost, is a balloon-capsule flight to the stratosphere, where you would not be in space or experience weightlessness but would see the Earth as one would see it from space, watching a whole day pass from above, day to night, and the blue Earth below you.

The motto for the arc flight I found online: Real Life, Minus Gravity.

On this father's second-to-last day, before our talk of outer space, he was shouting, true. Are you trying to kill me? But I am not the one he was shouting at. I had asked him if he wanted the things we were doing to him to stop. Sometimes, I said, a patient will tell us enough is enough.

Time you spend in certain rooms, brief permanent time, profound from all angles. As I turn it and turn it, I wonder if the problem is physical or philosophical. What the difference would be. This is just grief, of course, and everyone with whom I share this story—it is my first time being accused of murder—identifies with the son straightaway. This is grieving, they say, the story caught, summed up, named. But I am afraid of what is lost. So I look inside to find if I have killed anyone. My time in that room reminds me of only one other place I have ever been, another room I passed through that afterward I needed to tell everyone about, everyone I ever met for the rest of my life, and each time failed, though everyone thought right away they knew what I was talking about.

The past is permanent, is what I am trying to say. It comes to be something you can manage only because it does not change. But for this same reason, you can tell that the past is not real, because everything real changes all the time. In the process of becoming, nothing pauses long enough for you to get a handle on it.

One morning in the palliative-care unit I am checking in with the nurse. The patient in thirty-four, she says, looks close. So I go in and see a man who is dead already. Peaceful, eyes closed, hands folded across his chest. I declare him and go to tell the nurse, but I cannot find her. So I call the daughter myself. She is calm, which is rare but not unheard of. At some point in the call, the nurse runs in, waves her arms in and out of the shape of an X. She whispers sharply that she meant another patient was close to dead and still was only close—this one had gone an hour ago. She has already made the bereavement call. I stumble quickly through another round of condolences. When I get off, the nurse is laughing. What did you tell her? I say, I told her that I had an update. That we checked, and her father is still dead.

This is my dead father. I tell the funeral director I want to see the body. He is also the county coroner, a fact implying correctly the smallness of the county. I cannot always tell when he is speaking to me in which capacity. I meant to just see my father as is, on a slab somewhere. The body has not been embalmed; the casket will not be open. For context, I share that I am a medical professional. I have seen all kinds of things, I want to say but do not, cautious not to argue too much for myself. I think of a time, though, that I followed a woman through her death into the harvest of her organs. She had suffered a devastating brain injury after an elective procedure. Her family found great solace in her prospects as a donor. How it works is that they take you to a holding area outside the operating room with your family gathered all around the bed, and one room away, the surgeons are scrubbed in, scalpels at the ready. The breathing tube is removed, and if you die quickly enough that your organs aren't injured by hypoxia or mounting toxicity (an hour or two, depending on protocols that vary by institution), they rush you to surgery. With a cut like a seam coming undone, they open you from neck to navel, pull out your organs precisely and fast, and toss them into bins of ice, their gloved hands all covered in blood. Above all this, staff from the organ-procurement office read aloud from a statement written by your family about your strength and character, your love of life and faith in God. These, I mean, are the kinds of worlds I have moved between already. People I have cared for have been taken apart.

They hold my father's body in a walk-in for a little more than a week. We cannot leave right away. He has died between our two doses of the first vaccine. So he is placed in a freezer, what the coroner calls a temperature-controlled space. He has to wait until we get the second shot. What we see when we arrive is a casket on a stage, the lighting foiled to make the man less gray. The suit is blue; the neck is wrong. A haircut, fresh, a crew cut almost, a single-length shave with the guard set at an inch and a half, done fast, various lengths of hair left all over. Why cut the hair, I ask the coroner, and then I realize he has not followed us, that we are alone in the room.

In part of my mind my grief is performed for Eli. It is not clear to me how much I am allowed, since I have lost only the idea of something I never had. I touch my father's hand. There is black blood in the nail beds. Why would that be? He is cold, cold as a fucking beer can—that is what he said about his own dead father, a man I never knew, another funeral I did not attend. I am afraid as I touch him—of what, I wonder, and then I know. I am afraid that I will catch his death. Then all I can think is: How will I ever leave? How will I ever get out of this room? It must be that Eli guides me out to the hall or wherever we go to wait while they close the box before the service starts. This is called the private viewing. On the invoice for the funeral, I will see we are charged five hundred dollars for this display. When I pick up the urn, days later, after the Mass and his time in the oven, this is when I cry until I cannot breathe. That's it, says a woman, the receptionist, who is also the wife of the funeral director, the coroner—why is everyone so many things? She talks to me like I am giving birth. Lowers me onto a low chair. The urn is a block of stone in my arms. What I think, stupidly, is: What have I done? Something done, done badly, some vital thing rendered unknowable forever.

A question no one ever asks around here is what happens to people after they die? I mean, you know, existentially. It seems as if it would be central, or just off central, to the work we do, but amid all the symptoms and physician infights and family support, death itself, that very moment, is the end point as far as our service is concerned. Afterward, not so much. What happens next? is a question I do hear often from families. Rarely they mean the literal process of a living body going dead, and I have a gentle speech to give in such cases. But more often they mean the after-death as a matter of administration, of logistics. The first time I ever got asked that, years ago as an intern in an intensive-care unit, working days and days of daylong shifts, the full twenty-four hours, I didn't know the answer. Standing beside the first person I ever declared dead. Can you imagine? How I must have stuttered, as I still often do when

I am caught in uncertainty: I don't know, but I am happy to find out. All you do, it turns out, is call a funeral home, whichever one you want, tell them almost nothing, promise the body is uninfectious and that you are not bankrupt, and they arrange the rest with the hospital morgue.

In mortality class one day we take a trip to such a place, to what the tour guide calls a funeral chapel, to get a more visual sense of the process. Our program director tells the tour guide that all of us fellows have been with the dead dozens of times, briefly at least, in the moments that we declared them. But those transient bodies are not quite corpses. A corpse is a thing that death has settled into. I look around the room at us, set apart together by this startling fact. The tour guide tells us about the chapel. It is primarily Jewish but serves all comers. It is one of only three nonprofit funeral homes in the country. She talks at length about death's logistics, the importance of recording things accurately on the death certificates. Date of birth, Social Security number. Level of education—why would that matter? A funeral director walks by the little room. Anthony, Anthony, she shouts. The tour guide. She has been so clear to us that she is specifically not a funeral director. Why is level of education on the death certificate? she asks. For statistical reasons, he says. Record-keeping.

The tour guide impresses upon us the steep cost of city funerals. Even the most modest cost a solid five figures. And that does not include the cost to open and close the grave, she says. How much do you suppose they charge to open and close the grave? Up to thirty-six hundred dollars, she says, citing by name a reputable burial ground in New Jersey. We try to form the looks on our faces into ones of disbelief. This place does good business in shipping bodies back to the Holy Land. The transported bodies, religiously unembalmed, are packed in dry ice and escorted by a watcher. It is not as if every flight you take has a body, she says. But they do fly commercial.

What do the watchers do? was another question I wondered until it was asked out loud by someone else. The body would be under a drape, and the watchers would recite psalms of a peaceful journey or say the name of the deceased, the Hebrew name, which somehow prepared them for the trip. When it arrives where it is going, the body is washed in a ritual way—no small talk, says our tour guide, only prayers. The prayers here are taped to the wall in the washroom. The script is calligraphic, each letter a small box of hard straight lines. I wonder what they add up to. After the washing, each body is wrapped in a shroud, always the same sort of shroud, stitched by hand, each body wrapped and placed in a wooden box with wooden pegs for nails and wooden pegs set in wooden slides instead of metal hinges. Wrapped and boxed in just this way, there is no difference between us, she says. You cannot tell this one from that.

But why must they be washed and watched? The tour guide replies, with fantastic calm, that this is because the soul will hover around its body until it finds its place of rest. The soul is the watcher for the body, she says. And the watcher is watching that endeavor of separation. The performance of dignity is intended to say: All of this matters. She says this with such a granted manner, it is hard to find an objection. As for the haste? That time is such a turbulent time, she says. We want to get on with it. Get on with it—as purely, simply, and efficiently as possible. On the door of the refrigerator a printed sign reads:

ALL!!!!!!!!!!!!
REMAINS
MUST HAVE
HEAD BLOCK

The refrigerator is so loud that near it we cannot hear the tour guide. She gestures toward the chair where the watcher sits watching the refrigerator. He must be on a break. It's too loud, someone shouts. The refrigerator. The tour guide says, I know, but I probably should not try to adjust it.

I cannot picture this object, a head block. Later I find one on sale, online, for around fifty dollars. Terrible quality, says a review. The block rocks back and forth when heads are placed upon it! I do become instantly concerned about the length of time a dislodged soul might linger near its unburied body. The concern is acute. I have the ashes that once were my father in a box on a bookcase in the living room of my current apartment. After her speech about the watchers and the souls all floating around, she tells a sad and elaborate story about a member of her synagogue who died alone without anyone to notice and ended up unclaimed and buried in a trench on Hart Island. When the synagogue she attended found out, they moved heaven and earth, mostly the latter, to disinter her and bathe her and watch her and bury her properly, in wood, with the shroud. I ask the tour guide what might happen if a body never got where it was supposed to be buried, never got buried at all, if it got waylaid, say, permanently, in a bag in a box on a bookcase. She waves her hands. She does not believe in cremation. Anyway, if the bookcase is where he was going, she says, then he is already there. That is his final disposition. Disposition in this work is not an inclination or a tendency but rather a goal, a destination. Like all of the language, you get used to this with time.

After a few weeks ill at ease, listening at night for what I assume would be a faint rustling in the air of the living room, I ask a rabbi I work with to clear up this soul stuff a little. No one, he asks, is Jewish in this scenario? But he was alone, I say, and when he was just a body, the body was alone. And now instead of being in the ground, he is somewhere he would never want to be. I had even, after the move, moved the box to a lower shelf, the bottom shelf, actually, far from anyone's line of sight, even Sarah's. She is mesmerized by the box anytime it comes into her mind. I had—why?—told her it contained, in some way, my father, determined to gently answer any question she might ask. But now she cites him as an example whenever someone mentions an object that is lost, used up, or discarded. Some way into her time with us, she develops a persistent fear that physical harms will befall her body. She works hard to avoid all rough-and-tumble scenarios arranged by her age-matched playmates. Yet when she does trip or fall or otherwise sustain an injury, she is delighted, fascinated, most of all if the skin breaks—you will catch her gazing at the bandage intently, unsticking it to peer into the wound, smiling faintly for reasons she cannot or will not elaborate.

This rabbi is a chaplain in our department. He tells me that in Hebrew they use different words for the bodies of the living and the bodies of the dead and have another word for the actively dying, the liminal bodies, the ones on their way out the door. And three words for soul, he says sort of gleefully but does not tell me what they are. He will not let me get worked up about restless ghosts. The watching, the cleansing, have no implications for the soul's disposition. It is mostly a matter of respect, or the absence of respect, he says. That the consequences of a bad death, a bad burial, befall only the bereaved. Somewhere amid all this, I realize what I am asking: If you are a bad person, is there anything you can do about it if you are already dead? He suddenly looks at me as if I were a child. The weight you feel, he says, is not a need to forgive anyone. Just call it grief. Call it trauma. This isn't rabbinical, but it may be, though, at that moment when the soul comes loose, he says, in these moments a person can do the last of his work. Work like what, I ask him. If ghosts are real, he says, this is the time you might choose to become one. I suddenly do not know what kind of rabbi I am dealing with. I go home and look it up. I read some Deuteronomy. It seems that in the Jewish faith, ghosts may exist, but you aren't allowed to talk to them.

I think for a while that I will play a trick on myself regarding my dead father. I will tell myself he was a wonderful man. I use whatever memories I have of his joy and reposition them, reshape them, so that it appears he is joyful because of something good or morally right, or that he is happy with me, or with some neutral beauty, a view of the landscape on a summer night, the lights from the dock repeating in the soft waves on the lake. There is a problem, though, with the quality of the memories I have, with their duration. Lined up together in his absence, they suddenly reveal that I was always only walking in on him, catching him unaware: on the toilet, at the piano, once on the couch, crying about the dramatic end of a nature documentary. All of this was my fault, it seems, or the fault of a trouble I had, I have, an uneasiness with knocking on doors to announce myself. I find it somehow embarrassing to knock on one with no one behind it. Embarrassment requires, doesn't it, that second party? This continued to be an issue in my training as a doctor. The doors are now people, the knock is a voice: Open your eyes. Or the knock is still knuckles, rubbed hard into the sternum. The world is the closed door, says some mystic, a barrier, and at the same time it is the way through. Once, yes, I walk in on my father playing the piano. After he dies, in the shipwreck of his life, I find the piano in that same place, covered in dust and badly out of tune, a very large and merely decorative object. But my father used to play. The trouble with walking in is that because you are not expected, whatever you encounter tends either to change or to end quite abruptly upon your arrival. You, unwanted, have ended it. The quality, the duration of the experience— already so constricted by severe and sudden closure— become further distorted by this tone of rejection. The memories opacify and take on a quality of unreality at once. Heard in memory, in underwater time, the song he played expands and glorifies, it fills the room and my heart and his heart; in that moment before he sees me, we are both transformed.

Maybe the Bardo

I can see clearly in my mind the study in my father's first house. The furniture all so large, as it would appear to a child. The Bahamas desk, the curve of it, the color like that of the trunk of a palm tree, the chair a cabana backed in rattan. On the desk is a statue of an elephant with a canopied seat. In the seat is a smooth oblong rock he tells me is an egg. Under the desk is a thin square of hard rubber with teeth that hold on to the rug, so the cane legs of the chair can slide without sticking, to move with the movements of a large man, up and out. The ledger on the desk. He tells me this is where he writes his dreams. All of these things, the Bahamas desk, the elephant, the egg, are adrift in the dank basement at the lake house when he is dead and I go to clean up his life, put it away. The place may as well be underwater, the wreckage of a sunken ship. I find the ledger in a rubber tub in the mudroom. I have never touched it in my life. The page it opens to is marked with a plastic hospital bracelet. It is the last entry, years old, dated in an early month the year before the virus. If this were a drama on television, the ledger would reveal some deep meaning or great scandal. But what I see on the marked page is like notes you would write in the night upon waking from a dream. Piecemeal, illegible. I close the book and take it with me.

I see him once, my father, in the living room of his first house, the one with the study, asleep in the daytime with both his eyes open. I am a little child, maybe five. I stand a body's length away, regarding him for a long time, unseen, allowed, watching him breathe. The feeling that wells inside me is terror. When I leave the room, I run.

I sometimes wonder if the problem with Eli is related somehow to his infancy. He was born quite prematurely in a time when preterm birth was hard to survive. He spent the early months of his life in a hospital, largely untouched and unconsoled, in a plastic box, his arms tied down to protect IVs. He survived in part because despite his gestational age, he was uncommonly large, and he grew to be much taller and broader than you would expect if you ever laid eyes on his parents. I saw in an educational series that in the eighties it was commonly believed preterm infants could not feel pain, so doctors and nurses would perform procedures on them without any kind of analgesia or anesthesia, place lines or circumcise or even open their bodies for surgery. I imagine little Eli with his arm tied to a board. If he tried to suck his thumb, he would hit himself in the face. So he learned with his little body, right away, things that are true but that you should not learn anyway: that nowhere is safe, that no one is coming to comfort you.

I know this, too. The only remnant value is tenderness, the tenderness of foxholes, of sinking ships. And although we now work, in our own ways, in palliation, I don't know why we find so little for each other. The father at the monastery, the one whose son could not see the point of being alive. I was like that, too, at his age. Alive and suicidal. Do I say that to the father? Yes, I tell him. I say in my case the treatment was meaningful work.

Eli believes there is no point in making assertions. I have come home questioning freedom of the will. I start explaining to him the origin of consciousness in the bicameral mind, that we learned to speak, to be ourselves, to have selves, first from hearing the chatter of the dominant hemisphere. But isn't that all you are doing now, he says. Talking to yourself?

One summer when I am a young teenager I live with my father at that lake house. He works a lot and I am almost always alone. In an unclear sequence of events I get involved with a much older boy, a man, basically, because he has a car and can come out to the lake and collect me. There is something strange about him, about his body. Whenever I am close enough to him to hear his heart, I note that he exhales in two segments, pausing when his heart beats. I always do that, he says, I just do. This cannot be true, it cannot be constant. Who could live like that, breathing with pauses for the heartbeat? The fight I start about this ends our—whatever it is. He says: Something about you is seriously wrong. I remember looking out the window of his car at a huge early moon as he drives me back to the lake. This is the last time, he says, the last few times. We are not doing this again.

For not long, a day, a week, I consider keeping the lake house, and as I lie awake at night I imagine how to set it right. What to do with such low ceilings? The carpet would come out right away. I shift the walls, enlarge the kitchen and the side windows. I remember the house when he bought it. Even at the age I was, middle school, I approached the house with a curious sort of disappointment. Before that moment I had thought he was quite wealthy. A fireplace at the last house, orange-juice concentrate, extra rooms called pantries or mudrooms or studies. The mudroom at the lake house, though, did not contain galoshes in rows and baskets full of sunscreen and insect repellent. He was using it as a bedroom, the second of only two, the bed with no headboard, the place I was to sleep on the weekends when I was visiting. The carpet was thin and the floors felt hollow when you walked on them and the air was always cold.

I sometimes forget that he is dead and in forgetting bring him entirely back to life. In my own life, at least, which he has not been a part of in any real way in the decades since my childhood, there is no other difference between him alive and dead other

than how I think of him. So each time I remember,
I kill him again. He is the one who calls the heart
a prison. This is the only time he and Eli will
ever meet. My father is taking Eli's family history.
The men he drinks with call him the doctor, so
preoccupied is he with the complaints of the body,
the flaming joints, the halting bowels. He is concerned to learn that the men in Eli's family all have
bad hearts, bypass by fifty, best-case scenario. The
heart is a prison, he says, but he must mean blood,
genetics. As I render the details, they bend and fade,
like veins in an old arm, evading the needle. I see Eli
grow older, approach the date, his hair turning from
brown to gray, gray to white, out and up from the
temples. This isn't working, he likes to say, over and
over and over.

Brother Emptiness cautions us: Do not mistake
certainty for truth.

No Trumpets

Hope, in the Buddhist tradition, is not a virtue but a vice, a longing for life to be other than it is. Attachment to an imagined future is a rejection of things as they are. I believe this but have never said it aloud to a patient or a patient's family member, though I can imagine a situation in which I might say it, in which it might be useful. I am watching a woman watch her wife die from decompensated alcoholic cirrhosis. The woman in the bed is yellow—the bodies of white people become almost fluorescent when bilirubin from the failing liver builds up in the tissue. She is asleep and rouses only rarely to look around at nothing and moan.

It is spring. A slow end, cirrhosis; often it lingers terribly on and on. The yellow skin, the bones pulling through. The belly full of fluid, ascites, in a tense round shape like pregnancy. The woman has stringy hair and hazy sunken eyes—she looks like someone you would see on the street or in the dirt by the road in a film set in the Middle Ages, a leper or a keeper of some other frightening contagion. But her wife shared a photograph, and there she is, just months ago, a normal-appearing woman, not unhandsome, smiling into the lens. Something happened to her in lockdown. She had always been the life of the party, her wife says, but alone at home it took a turn, and then it was hepatitis and now this. Her liver failed, and she is dying. She is not the first I have seen, people whose coping is catching up to them. Even someone from my hometown, my own age, drank himself to death that first summer of the virus. Others overdosed on street drugs or shot themselves or shot somebody else. The day that will be the day she dies, I am walking into work. The sunrise is newly early enough that there is full light when I walk across the park, and the air is cold and the light is good and the trees are just getting green along the bends and ends of the branches. The wife has been at vigil for weeks. And I have this feeling, on the sidewalk, which is almost not a feeling but a wide utter blank, just the scene, the trees, being on the right side of the walls, out of the bed. And I know that soon that wife will walk away and feel this too, and that will be all. That the reward of the labor of our love is this.

There won't be any trumpets blowing, I guess is what I am getting at. Early on, the psychologist tells me with some insistence that the goodness of the world is at least commensurate to the bad. This does not hold up to scrutiny as a fact, but it also cannot be proved wrong. Though there are plenty of people who have witnessed atrocities, have seen bodies cut up and hanging from the trees, and still they will agree that trees are beautiful; plenty who have passed through the fire, who are badly scarred, permanently marked, who can do as I do, feel as I feel when I look at those first budding leaves. It doesn't mean anything. But this is the note of triumph: It doesn't mean anything!

On the train I read in a magazine about a man who murdered his two young children. The article begins framed not around him but around another man, a lettuce farmer who, led by barking dogs, found the little bodies behind a fence, lying in a dry creek bed. The farmer saw the little feet first, two feet and then three, the fourth tucked up under the pale body of the little one, dressed in just a diaper and the desert dust. They run with the article a printed photo of the spot where the bodies were found, with small crosses of rough white pine and the two names written in marker, a kerchief laid with stones or shells, and small bright ojos de dios, sticks woven with yarn. The journalist, in stories like this, tries of course to make sense of it, attributing the father's gruesome acts to belief in far-right conspiracy theories. Why didn't he just leave them with me? the farmer is quoted as asking. I would have taken them, without anything.

I write a letter to an old friend and don't hear back for months. When he does write back, the reply begins: Sorry for the delay, I have broken both of my arms.

Packages come in the mail addressed to me, but the notes inside fall under the name of someone else. One such package contains a book of photographs. It pictures every known animal that has gone extinct since the invention of photography. A note in blue ink falls from between the pages. It reads: There is a lot of interest in this space!

The day I reopen my father's ledger is no particular day. It is a day far enough from his death that the shape of the man in my head has changed entirely, and the living one is wholly effaced. Tucked between the pages of the ledger are letters from women who have left him, letters in which at great length they elaborate the reasons he is intolerable. Mostly the drinking and drinking so much that he would yell or break things, crash a car, urinate on the sofa in his sleep. There is a letter from a friend, a soldier overseas, apologizing for a misread gesture toward his second wife: I thought you and I were good, it says, but from what I hear you are somewhere else in your thoughts. Tucked in with the letters are golf-course scorecards, newspaper clippings, some artifacts of my childhood, drawings of mine and my brother's that our mother must have mailed him. My handwriting, age five. It could be any child's, though it shows already some of the tendencies it will maintain forever, a carelessness, an upward drift, never touching the lines. This is a made-up world, it reads, scrawled over something like a map, green and orange and yellow shapes drawn onto a crayon expanse of blue. A postscript on the back says: Sorry it is not very good.

Cleaning out his house, I find on his desk a note-pad where he has written my name, current address, and occupation. I find the first letter my mother wrote him after that accident, the one that changed everything: My dear, what have you done?

She says she has heard he gives the nurses a hard time—they have to keep him medicated to make him behave. She describes me, an infant, frowning and furrowing my brow: my father's look of disgust. I tell her about you, she writes. I tell her that no matter how things turn out, it will always be okay to love you. I do not really know why she leaves him. The answer is not here, and she never quite told me, though I know he is the reason she cannot breathe through her nose. From the moment of the letters it is clear she regrets it, that she wants the marriage to come back together. What are your dreams, she writes. Perhaps you would wish for enough money that you would never have to worry. Or perhaps you just want the years back. The years, I think. There were not many. These letters are addressed to the intensive-care unit where he lived for months after the accident. After the first time they speak on the phone, after the wires have been removed from his jaw, she writes to him: I talk too much, I say the wrong things. I want you to like me a little. A later date, another letter from another woman, calling things off. It reads: Perhaps if you were happier, you wouldn't drink so much.

The section in the ledger labeled DREAMS contains very few. Who knows what I had been hoping for. In one, my father recounts playing partnered tennis with Joseph Stalin. He struggles with his serve. If I double-fault one more time, he writes, he will send me off to the gulag. Someone in the crowd shouts: Think of the children! Stalin plays tennis in his dress whites, my father notes, the same outfit he wore at Potsdam. In another dream, my parents have bought a new house sight unseen. *My parents*—I seldom collect them together in this phrase. The new house is grand and enormous, with high ceilings and marble floors, stained-glass windows everywhere, the living room the size of a gymnasium. But a man comes in after them with a high-caliber rifle and starts shooting. My father tells my mother to call the police, but she will not. She says the police make her feel foolish. All the rest of the dreams are about drugs and drinking and violence. In one he and his next wife smoke opium until semiconscious and then comes someone they have hired to slit their throats.

I often dream of better houses, too, or of new rooms in old houses, rooms I have never noticed in houses where I have lived for years. A hole appears in the wall or a door never seen opened suddenly comes to light, opens to a small room, long, narrow, dark. Often the walls are unfinished or crumbling, plaster loose on the laths. Sometimes the room is filled with an array of old and broken furnishings, torn paintings in large gilded frames, antiquated radios, all coated in the same fine dust that rises from dirt floors in the basements of ancient houses. The sensation of discovery is in any case a rush of joy like a chill over the body. Finally! A contentless relief.

And I dream of my father often, too, after his body is burned and I bring him home. Brutal dreams, lifelike and set in his house. In the first one, I am coming up the stairs from the basement room where I'd slept that summer, and I see him sitting at the table with his head leaning on his hand. And I am so relieved, so overwhelmed with relief, that he is not dead and that I can tell him—tell him what? Until I see it is just his body, his corpse, propped up at the table. In another, he is helping me clear out his things. I do not like for him to see what I have chosen, placed little orange stickers on, the objects I want to keep. I wonder if his presence means I should stop sorting out and disposing of his whole material life. Eventually I try to ask him. He doesn't remember dying or the funeral or any of it. I explain to him that he was clearly dead the last time I saw him. In the dream he has his old hair, gray and overgrown and pushed back. But when I saw him in the casket, his hair was white and all cut short for some reason. I tell him this, in the dream, about the haircut. Then he seems to remember. He laughs. Oh yeah, he says, what the fuck was that?

Typed and tucked into the ledger there is a manuscript, apparently a draft of a novel. On the first page is etched a title in clumsy ballpoint script. Midway through the draft, improbably, I find a description of the sudden death of the protagonist's father, a beloved tyrant, from an unwitnessed heart attack one night in his chair. The text reads: And he died alone, the way death should always be. He liked to be alone in it. This was his last thought.

In the days after I go through the ledger, I feel a broad blankness that is a peaceful cognate of disappointment, the feeling of finding things just as they are. It flattens even further with a few nights of sleep. And what rises in that blankness is a new page, a favorite: surrounded by blank pages, like a one-off, a note addressed to my mother. The writing is a wide inebriated scrawl. It says that my mother must live her dreams, learn to paint, and do all the cultural things that mean so much to her, and that he, my father, must also make art and make music. I must get back, he writes, to the piano. Wake me up soon, he signs off. I am thrilled to no end!

In the End

The last time through the hospice unit, I find that when I first approach the patients, they occur to me as forms, as roles, as presentations: whatever age, skin tone, whatever shape is carved out of them from this or that specific illness. There is a horror and an ease, equal parts, to seeing the patients in this way, though with a little effort, I find I can shift my perspective. The effort is this: I consider the person's face, and then my own, the thought of my own, the thought that I, too, seem to be a face presented to the others. And then the whole mysterious world fills the space between our faces. How can I help, I ask a woman with heart failure who comes in every month with fluid in her lungs, with the sensation of drowning, who is delirious, tied to the bed. You cannot help me, she says, in Russian, so I have to wait for the interpretation. You are an idiot, illiterate doctor. Send me home if you only wish to harm me. When I listen to her chest, what I hear beating is the same heart she had as a child.

I describe my approach in the last session of mortality class, but I seem to get the words wrong. It is okay, the classmates say, to see a death and feel nothing. It is not our own, everyone separately says. The life, I guess they mean. The grief? You are performing a service—what matters is the service itself, not the way you feel about it.

The splitter dies, and the woman with ALS dies, and the surgeon with all the suits. Someone tells me this—I am no longer their doctor, always rotating off, always someplace else. Did he ever make it home? Certainly never back to work. But I do not look back on the chart to find out. What difference could it make? Sometimes I learn of particular deaths in the news or in a newsfeed online, and there will be a photograph, like of an old couple, smiling in the kind of posed studio portraits that no one does anymore, who died alone together in the first wave, loving mother, loving father. And it escapes belief for a moment, those faces, those singular deaths, in the startling violence of scale. Constantly shifting points of view between the two of them and the million others has no other function than to disorient.

I tell Eli about the death scene in my father's book, but there are other things in it I do not tell anyone. There is something in it I do not know what to make of—I suspect it is just bigoted trash, then wonder dumbly if it holds a key to a problem I have been living with. My mother appears in the book; the character is clearly her, even has her childhood nickname as an actual name, but unlike my mother in actual life, in the book she is transgender. She passes quite well except for her large hands and a singular air, a strangeness the protagonist often remarks on. The situation comes to light when she proves incapable of bearing children. Then there is a moment of slapstick horror for the protagonist, who suddenly finds he has been for some time in love with and married to and sleeping with, he exclaims, a man. From his point of view the horror is only gay panic: She is a man! She is a man! It seems quickly obvious to me that my mother appears that way in the book because of how my father came in time to be disturbed by attributes of hers that he considered masculine: intelligence, selfishness, indeference. She did of course bear him children, one of whom now appears to be a woman and will not bear children and is me, having a hard time. But maybe he meant only that there was something deeply wrong with her and he did not know what it was.

Indeference, it turns out, is not a word. The opposite of deference is noncompliance.

When I was a child, my mother taught me that if you apologize for something and then do it again, it proves you are not sorry. I understood this to mean it is not possible to know whether you are sorry until sufficient time had passed. And since over time I have come to note that I am not in control of my actions, who am I to report on whether or not I am sorry, will go on to prove sorry, as life continues playing out upon us? I do not throw things anymore, though the fact that I used to comes up often, that I am violent, selfish, and noncompliant. I also do the bulk of the housework, though when I am done with fellowship and fully a doctor with the salary the job entails, I will pay someone to do housework for me. A woman, I am sure.

It is my last week of work when I begin to feel ill. The home tests are negative but for the past few waves, they always are. I have lost so much time to false alarms—the test day and the day after, every time, and a few more days waiting for the call from Employee Health that never came until I was back at work for days already when they would clear me. The past few scares I just worked through, allergies, probably, psychogenic dyspnea. I turn my head to cough into my shoulder, and during a meeting I feel the onset of fever as the faces around me begin to change, to grow long and spin about their mouths, and suddenly it matters not at all to me if their aunt had really known what she was saying before this stroke, this coma, when she said to keep her on machines forever. I should leave right away, I realize all at once, but this is my last day of work, and it is over.

It has happened already, a thousand times before, that certain weakness, an ache, a dryness to the eyes. The tests used to be so hard to come by, you would have to stand for hours and hours in line, so instead I would just hate life in my body, a life I knew I was oversensitive to, and choose to just go to work instead of missing a week because of another bout of vague symptoms. But now Sarah is gasping and coughing until she gasps, and Eli looks pale, and now the home tests we have come to hoard come up positive right away, one after another. I am not shocked and not afraid—we have been vaccinated years running, we are otherwise well, we are not the kind of people who die of this. What fear I feel is like a memory of fear, like being out in a cabin in the woods as the night sets in, the real dark night of the country, and remembering that the dark would frighten me if I were alone, but I am not. Whatever fear comes after that feels performed somehow, re-cited. So we lie low, get groceries delivered, and sleep off our shared fevers, timing Tylenol and watching television.

Over our long quarantine I have a sense of the illness as a duty long put off. I am the least sick by a few days in and vaguely elated, in love somehow with Eli or Sarah, our family holed up together in-doors like denned animals. I am the one well enough to walk the dog, sneaking in mask and gloves out of the building, the fresh air keeping me from losing my mind. The path up to the woods is just across from the apartment, and the woods are mostly empty on weekdays. The entrance is a hill steep enough for sledding when the snow comes. But this is high summer, the whole world a fever. I like to walk the hill to know I am not so short of breath. I am trying not to think of all the people I have seen on vents, one especially, my same age and vaccinated, who died of a huge blood clot in the lungs from the strange thing the virus does to your blood. It has just been a holiday weekend, and the woods are full of trash. I keep passing on this daily walk something that looks like a body. It is far enough off the trail that it is hard to say the size, a rounded shape shrouded in a blue blanket coming out from behind the edge of an old stone wall. Now I am seeing the dead everywhere.

As Sarah and Eli begin to recover, I take them out on my walk with the dog. When we pass the wall I point out, self-consciously, what surely is not a dead body. Then the dog darts toward it, and we notice it is covered in flies. Up closer I see that the pale blue blanket is knotted in a ball the size of a child. It makes me dizzy to see it, the bulk of it, the flies, like the world is spinning, as if I cannot breathe. It is Eli who knows what to do, who calls the police, who tries to explain. They take hours to come and arrive brusque and skeptical. I see the guns and stay away. I watch from the apartment, the front windows, see Eli and the policemen as little men far up the green hill. For Sarah I try to seem calm, try not to seem to be staring out the window. Another police car arrives; there are four officers now, leaning on the cars to offset the weight of their belts. After forever, a man in gloves walks up to the tree. I can see him only a little. I flee from the window. Eli's face as he enters the house is unreadable. He comes through the door and sighs, then coughs. He says it was somebody's dog.

I lie awake long into the night, listening for Sarah. I hate to think of that dog's last days, says Eli, convinced the abandoned body meant a violent end. I do not know what it means. I can imagine someone, wrongheaded in grief, someone alone, maybe older, who perhaps wanted to dig a hole in the woods to bury a dog who died at home of natural causes. It is easy to imagine wanting to, and then the dog being too heavy, the hill too steep. I can imagine someone who could not imagine how hard it would be until he started to climb. But what really sets me off, what disturbs me in my body, is something I know now, now that I have watched the officer in gloves move to where I cannot see him from the window. I know what it feels like to live in a world where you can find a dead child tied up under a tree.

I hear Eli breathing the way he breathes when he is asleep. I do not turn toward him or reach out to touch him, but I am glad he is there. The truth is I would like to be left under a tree. Buried, I mean, straight in the dirt. Kept from the knives and the fires, kept from the men at the eye bank. There is a place you can do that, where you must, in fact, come in fresh and not be embalmed, be wrapped up only in cloth. It is upstate, and your people can even fill the hole in after you, though the cemetery website cautions that closing a grave is harder than you might imagine. The soil is dense and full of stones. It takes large, able-bodied parties to close the grave themselves. I want this, though who knows if I will have the friends for it. I want to go and see the place. Eli says not to take Sarah to a graveyard, though it is not a graveyard, because there are not any graves. Or graves are where the bodies go—but there are no headstones. They allow only flat rocks to mark where the bodies are, and even the rocks must be native to the region. The field is marked with a hand-painted sign like one that might announce a flea market, green letters shadowed in silver.

A young chaplain at Eli's work is a Buddhist monk, from a line of monks who follow in the steps of the great Buddhist saints and meditate in the charnel grounds in India, where the bodies of the dead are laid out under the sun to bloat and be picked apart by crows. If you get through the morning forgetting that you will die, he says, the morning has been wasted. But Manhattan is low on charnel grounds, and the monk doesn't travel by air. That is why, he says, I have come to work in the hospital.

In the interval between giving a dose of intravenous opioids and seeing the peak effect, I will sometimes pass the time by catching up on the news. There is almost always a disaster imminent, some new variant, more virulent, more insidious, spreading somewhere else in the world. You get used to it, watching the gathering reasons to be afraid, and be afraid, and do nothing—even when the threat is at the door. And the world goes on like always, one day a new war, a nuclear threat, a rocket in uncontrolled free fall spinning toward the planet. It will hit the sea, says a night nurse with solemn confidence. She wears a scrub skirt instead of pants, suggesting an unspecified religiousness requiring a firm expression of gender. The name of the rocket I remember wrong as Far from Home. Do I lose sleep as it falls? Do I lie in bed at night feeling the growing rumble, picturing the late bright light? Somewhere a man wears an EEG when he happens to suddenly die, and after his heart stops, what fires off in his brain are the oscillatory patterns of inward focus and re-call, remembering: life flashed before his eyes. What will I see, I wonder, anything more than these thou-sand-thousand fearful moments, alone, the physical sensations of being afraid, a tight chest, a burning in the hands and arms? And what else? Some socialists I know say we gave up on public health because the public needs to learn to go about in these conditions, eating and shouting and spending money, because the near future will be full of mass death, already there is nothing to be done about it.

A journalist asks a monk how he can pray for compassion in a world he knows nothing about, living with no access to the internet or television. There had just, for example, been a shooting in a grade school in which the victims were mostly children under the age of seven. The monk reflects: I am familiar with the concept.

We mostly recover from the virus, though we are all dizzy for weeks after, dizzy when we stand up, and Sarah is always falling into walls and laughing. Eli cannot breathe right for a long time, cannot ride his bike for a month on account of his lungs, which makes him housebound and sour. My training is over, and I am done, an expert, I guess, in pain and symptom management. I find a job in the city where they make me swear never to say the word *death* until I am asked to. But I still think it over, still want to, still want to learn to face it bravely. The shroud, the ground, you could not tell me apart from any other. Maybe as they fill the hole, a cellist could play Bach in the grass. Write it down, Eli tells me, write it down. Whatever else I might deride Eli for, this is a task he will execute perfectly: weighty, finite, elaborately predefined. I can see him there, standing tall among our strong and faceless friends. How handsome, standing in dirt near the hole with a shovel, dirt on his shirt and up his arms. And you, if you go first, I ask. He says it doesn't matter. So I will give him what I want. Between then and now he will stay with me, no matter what he says. I think he will stay. I hope he does.

If only we could find a home someplace on Earth that could stand for our whole lives, the right side of the right hill, safe from the fires and the water's rise. Or if we could just commit to unextraordinary wanting and sate it a little—is this a high-end lamp, a place outside the city, another child to keep up with Sarah? See it all, and call it something else. There are days where the dawn breaks so bright it seems there is no more sorrow. Then there are days it weighs in the air: the looming accident, the unknown illness, waiting, just waiting. Oh, it is only a bruise. It is only a headache.

Acknowledgments

Continued and unending gratitude to the people whose support made this work possible: Stephen Douglas, Garielle Lutz, Sarah Burnes, Sophie Pugh-Sellers, Vivian Lee, Morgan Wu, Elizabeth Garriga, Jayne Yaffe Kemp, Tracy Roe, Amy Hempel, Jenny Offill, Miranda Popkey, Max Reynolds, Edie Meyerson, Diane Meier, Eugene Choi, Catherine Varner, Lilyth Varner, Nicholas DeForest, and Peter Chamberlin.

About the Author

Anna DeForest is the author of the novel *A History of Present Illness* and a palliative-care physician in New York City.